WINDOW OF TIME

WINDOW OF TIME

OLIVIA L. OLSON

This book is a work of fiction. However, several names, descriptions, entities, and incidents included in the story are based on the lives of real people.

Published by Tate Publishing & Enterprises, LLC
127 E. Trade Center Terrace | Mustang, Oklahoma 73064 USA
1.888.361.9473 | www.tatepublishing.com

Tate Publishing is committed to excellence in the publishing industry. The company reflects the philosophy established by the founders, based on Psalm 68:11,

"The Lord gave the word and great was the company of those who published it."

Cover design by Joana Quilantang
Interior design by Shieldon Alcasid

Published in the United States of America

ISBN: 978-1-68164-341-0
Fiction / Historical
16.03.04

Contents

Libby's Discovery 7
Quinn's Discovery 17
Peter's Discovery 46
Rosalie's Discovery 55
Etta's Discovery 68
Wyatt's Discovery 78
Scarlett's Discovery 110
Bennett's Discovery 129

Bibliography 143

Libby's Discovery

February 9
Present Day

THE THERMOMETER READ 103 degrees Fahrenheit. Juliet's cheeks were scarlet. While Grandma Libby drew water for a tepid bath, the child cradled in her arms grew limp. Soothingly, she gave a kiss on her forehead and whispered, "God loves you," a kiss on each hand, "mother and dad love you," and a kiss on each foot, "grandpa and grandma love you."

Juliet whimpered as Grandma Libby gently placed her into the water and spoke, "In you go, sweetheart, in you go."

Hours later, she rocked and sang Juliet into a peaceful sleep. The steady back-and-forth motion of the rocker drew Grandma Libby's thoughts back to her childhood and immediately she remembered the doll. The doll locked away in her special box on top of the bookshelf. The doll with a story all its own.

July 5, 1935

"Thank you, Dub, these blackberries will make a fine cobbler!"

Alerted by a car on the gravel driveway, Olive wiped the boy's brow with her apron and dusted off her flour-covered hands to see who the unexpected caller could be. Before a knock was on the door, she opened it. "Why, Judge McMurtrey, won't you come in?"

"Good day, Miss Olive, little Dub," he said as he nodded to her and her youngster. "I've come here strictly on business because there's no one else I'd rather see take this job."

"Well, Judge, Wallace is down at the shop, and he won't be home 'til suppertime," Olive responded.

"No, no. It's not Wallace I came to see," he paused. "It's you. The government has started sewing rooms across the county to employ women. Miss Cornelia Lee in Little Rock called and asked if I knew anyone in the area who'd serve as director of the rooms for Rison, New Edinburg, and Kingsland. I told her you were the best woman qualified for the job."

"Oh now, Judge, you can see I've got my hands full here. I have Dub and little James to think of. But I'll talk to Wallace," she countered back.

"Well, your boys will be in school by the time they're in operation, and you can work your hours around their schedules. As for Wallace, I'm sure he'll agree to let you work," the judge said.

Six months later
Rison, Arkansas

Emogene Grady stared at the check Miss Olive handed her. After a long moment, she said, "I cain't believe it! How do I get money for it?" Emogene held the first paycheck she'd ever earned.

Olive smiled back with compassion and understanding. "Emogene, take the check to the Bank of Rison and sign your name on the back. They'll cash it for you."

Emogene answered barely above a whisper, "But I cain't write my name."

Motioning her away from the others, Olive took her aside and printed it in large letters on a separate sheet of paper. She slipped the paper into her hand, and said, "Emogene, here it is. Practice writing this over and over at home. Then once you feel ready, write your name on the back of the check, and the bank will cash it."

Olive's natural leadership and companionable approach with the ladies of the sewing rooms made her appointment well suited for her personality. In a small community such as this, her endorsement would naturally have followed the recommendation of peers. Likely from those who knew her role in the church or respected her strong belief in family. Career women in the 1930s were typically unmarried and lived in larger cities. However, this new program, Works Progress Administration, established by Franklin D. Roosevelt, began to change all that.

As the months slipped by, Olive grew closer to the ladies in each of the sewing rooms. Many, like her, were at work for the first time, but grateful to help their families through the difficult years of the Great Depression.

One stormy Thursday, Emogene walked up to Miss Olive and asked, "Mam, my husband Jim left me last night, and there's no one at home to watch my girl Violet. I took her by Miz Rutledge's place this morning, but she said she's too old to take care of little children…that I'd best find somewhere's else to take her tomarra. I, I don't know what to do. May I bring her with me in the morning, and let her play over yonder in the corner beyond the basters? I promise she'll be good and no trouble, at least 'til I can find someones else to watch her."

"Of course," Olive answered. "Later on, we can ask the ladies if they know anyone else who might be able to help you."

Following supper that evening, Olive picked up her phone receiver and dialed the operator switchboard, "Ida, ring Polly McAfee's number for me, will you?"

"Sure thing, Miss Olive," Ida answered back.

The next day, Polly, one of Miss Olive's basters and granddaughter, MaeLily, walked to the sewing room while they carried lunch pails and sang gospel songs.

As the workday progressed, Olive monitored each employee's needlework when she happened to glance in the corner where Violet and MaeLily played and marveled over their ingenuity. Both girls held a straight stick with crudely tied scraps of material on the top to pretend they were dolls. Suddenly, Olive had an idea. She knew it would take a little time and planning on her part, but with fabric pieces she'd been saving at home, she was confident she'd be able to complete her objective after Wallace and the boys finished supper and went to bed.

The next day, Olive glimpsed down at the timepiece on her brooch to signal the workday finished. She thought, *In half an hour, these ladies will all return home to begin their dinnertime meal.* Now, they pulled threads from the peddle machines, sorted scraps by size for later use on quilts or piecework, all while masking their noses and mouths as they swept and mopped the room spotless. Olive had lost her father ten years earlier from TB and was convinced the grime he breathed over the years was the blame. Wallace was always teasing her, "Olive, if you don't die of TB, you'll be disappointed you fear it so." Still, she wanted the ladies to be more cautious when they cleaned and not risk illness from dust particles they stirred up.

Over the next several evenings, Olive designed and made two cloth dolls. Originally, the dark material was to be MaeLily's and the lighter one, Violet's. But as she laid the cut cloth together for sewing, a brainstorm hit her. What if she made them two-sided dolls? Opposing colors of cloth on the front and back so the girls could pretend they were one another? What better way to remember that special day together in the sewing room than to have such a doll? *It hadn't been that many years since she was a little girl herself,* Olive smiled in recollection.

Monday afternoon Olive finished the inspection of the ladies tasks at the New Edinburg sewing room when she realized she'd have just enough time to drive back to Rison before that location closed. Inside her bag were two finished dolls; one she'd give to Polly for MaeLily, and the other to Emogene for Violet. Olive was pleased with herself as she thought over the dolls' details: embroidery on their faces as well as yarn tied with ribbon for hair. She was especially proud of the two-sided calico dresses she added when she tied the final knot.

Later, Olive walked into the Rison compound just as the ladies were in line to complete their workday. She spied Polly first and said, "Look, I've made a little something for the girls. I wish you'd give this to MaeLily and tell her I was so tickled to see she made friends with Violet. I want her to have this as a keepsake."

"Why, Miz Olive, that's so kind of you. She'll treasure this little doll, I knowz it. I'z only wish Miz Emogene wuz here for you to give her Violet's," Polly remarked.

"Well, where is Emogene?" Olive asked, suddenly aware as she looked around she hadn't seen her when she walked indoors.

"Oh, Miz Olive, I heard tell from one of them other ladies her girl Violet iz awful sick."

Olive knew Wallace would understand her delay at home when he heard why she'd driven out to the Grady place to check up on one of her ladies.

In a rush, she knocked on the screen door and realized she had forgotten the doll on the car's front seat. *Oh well,* she thought, *I'll run back out and get her before I leave.* However, what greeted Olive as she opened the door was the last thing she expected. Emogene appeared with red, swollen eyes and sobbed. "She's gone, Miss Olive, my little girl is gone!"

June 26, 1960

A metal box stood off to one side of a closet shelf until Olive's granddaughter, Libby, found it while she played dress-up with her grandmother's shoes, hats, and dresses.

Libby grabbed the box and carried it to her grandmother and asked, "Big Mom, what do you keep in here?"

"Oh my dear," Olive responded. "Let me get the key and we shall see."

As she unsecured the lock with a skeleton key, Olive opened the metal lid slowly, delighted by Libby's anticipation. Nestled beneath an embroidered pillowcase, was a most unusual two-sided doll. Olive held it up and said, "Why, I'd quite forgotten about her!"

And so Olive told the story of the doll to her granddaughter with all its portents of meaning.

In the end, she spoke, "You know, dear, by the time I left that sad house so long ago, I'd overlooked the doll until I came home and got out of my car. I determined right then I'd put her away. Many years later, I looked for a safe place to keep her and thought, 'Why not in the box along with my sewing ladies paychecks?'" Then she added, "Emogene never returned to the sewing room. I heard through the grapevine her Jim came home, and they moved to Texas."

Libby asked, "Do you know how Violet died?"

"Oh yes," her Big Mama answered. "She died of typhoid fever."

"You know, Libby, there's no need for me to keep this little doll. I'll give her to you as well as my special box and key. Maybe someday in the future, a young girl will come into your life that will bring a smile to your heart. Take out this doll, and give it to her."

February 10
Present Day

"Juliet, Juliet, wake up…you've been asleep a long time, and I know you feel better," she said as she touched her cheek. "Grandma Libby has a special surprise for you!" Then she placed Violet's doll into her arms.

******

I wrote this story to honor, Mary Olive Smith Hobson, "Libby's" grandmother, who was the director of the sewing rooms in Rison, New Edinburg, and Kingsland, Arkansas, during the WPA days of the 1930s. She later became the director for five counties to include: Cleveland, Dallas, Lincoln, Bradley, and Calhoun. Her responsibilities were not only for the sewing rooms but canning kitchens that put many women to work for the first time in their lives. "Miss Olive" as known by all those neighbors, friends, and locals, who knew her was an inspiration to many for the full ninety-six years of life she led. And so begins the *Window of Time* stories as Libby, the author, becomes a grandmother, passing down accounts and yarns she heard from her paternal and maternal grandmothers' in the 1950s and 1960s.

Quinn's Discovery

CHIMES ON THE mantel clock sounded the hour while Quinn imagined he struck a giant gong with the spatula in his hands. A burst of warm air jolted him back into reality. Oatmeal and spice wafted the air as Grandma Libby removed trays laden with cookies from the oven. *Yum*, Quinn thought, while he scooped the hot treats onto a plate.

His grandma wiped her hands on her apron and unfolded a large sheet of paper filled with lines and names arranged in a treelike fashion across an open spot on the table.

"What are you doing, Grandma Libby?" he asked.

"I'm just about finished with my family tree. Names over here are my mother's parents and grandparents, and names on the other side belong to my father's family. You know Quinn, each name represents someone with a unique story to tell."

His eyes swam over the tree drawn with an artistic flourish. On top of its leafy branches were lines placed neatly, filled with name after name in calligraphy script.

"Quinn, we're all given a window of time. No one else will share the exact experiences you've shared, nor will you see the world through the same lens as each one of these lives before you. But we get a glimpse into their lives when we study history the proper way."

Quinn could see the twinkle in her eye that begged his question.

"What is the proper way, Grandma?"

She leaned over beside him, and in a whisper-like voice said, "You've got to walk in their shoes. Tell yourself you no longer live in the twenty-first century, but go back in time to their day. I think of it as a mystery to be solved. Each name, especially the further back you go in generations, offers a variety of questions or puzzles that you, as the detective, must try to solve."

Quinn's grandma placed a plate of four warm cookies and two glasses of milk on the table. While he surveyed the family tree again, he scanned back and forth over different names and dates, most, still mysteries to him.

Randomly, he let his finger fall near two names of the same generation, but on separate lines, and queried, "Grandma Libby, do you know the story of Pur-nell Chance and William Killingsworth?"

"Why yes, those men were my great-great-grandfathers, your fourth great-grandfathers and both of them fought in the Civil War. Come here a moment to the living room, and I'll show you something."

On a bookshelf stood two soldierly figurines: one dressed in Union blue, mounted on a horse; the other in

Confederate gray, bearing a musket with a fixed bayonet by his side. "I bought these when I visited Gettysburg, Pennsylvania, several years ago. I've always pictured one as Corporal William J. Killingsworth of the Confederate States of America, the other as Private Purnell Chance, of the United States Cavalry.

"You mean they fought on opposite sides?" Quinn asked.

"Oh yes, and they both have quite a story to tell," she answered.

Just at that moment, Quinn's grandpa was heard coming through the backdoor drawn to the aroma of freshly baked cookies.

"Were you going to eat all these without me?" he teased.

Though distracted by the interruption, Quinn couldn't wait to hear more about the lives of soldiers who lived so long ago.

But first he'd join his grandpa in a horse-drawn cart for a ride around the fields and woods that surrounded the farm. Content to take in crisp fall air and the occasional perfume of red cedar, Quinn concentrated on sounds in the forest as the cart's wheels crackled over dry twigs along its path. The slow, steady pace gave him a perfect opportunity to conjure up soldiers behind trees, ready to ambush them.

I wonder which battles Purnell and William fought? he thought.

However, that question would be answered another day.

The following Saturday, Quinn found himself inside Grandma Libby's kitchen once again. Only this time she'd already prepared the cookies the night before.

"Quinn, today you're not only going to learn history, but you're also going to taste history!"

Intrigued, he let her continue.

"During the past week, I dug through all my old family recipes. Look up there," she said as she pointed to the shelf above him, "behind the brick I use for a bookend is my favorite book of recipes. And tucked inside was my great-grandmother's tea cake recipe. I made them last night, so as you savor one you might encounter the very flavors some of your ancestors enjoyed in the past."

Quinn sat down in front of the plate piled high with tea cakes. Across the table, he noticed a rectangular metal box with a skeleton key beside it. His curiosity, piqued.

While he swallowed the first bite, his grandma said, "Sweetheart, last week you asked me about Purnell and William. I'm going to let you in on a secret: my favorite author, Corrie Ten Boom once wrote, 'When you dig up the gold coins of the past, they must be beaten into useful coins for today.' History has valuable lessons to teach us if we're willing to dig long and hard enough to find them. Purnell and William were just ordinary men with families who loved them. However, they were caught up in a tumultuous period that forced them away from their families. Both men never returned home to see their little ones become adults or hold any future grandchildren."

As Quinn let this information sink in, the war's reality began to dawn on him. No longer was it the excitement of a battle's charge on a mounted horse or a parade of troops with gleaming weapons in their arms. Instead, he envisioned Purnell and William's lives cut short, each with a family expecting his return at war's end, and the devastation they felt when that didn't happen.

"Inside this box, Quinn, are documents," Grandma Libby continued as she pulled it toward him. "*Primary source documents* come from material written during their lifetime. One is a pension record for Purnell. In it are details that explain a little about his life and family. Purnell's pension revealed how his family collected payment for his service after his death. Before that, he'd been their only source of income. The other documents are old letters; some, between William and his family. I'll entrust these in your care to uncover any details you can about their lives. Be careful when you handle the old letters, they're fragile. Then next week, I'll look forward to hearing what you've discovered."

The following day, Quinn settled on top of the quilted coverlets of his bed and opened the documents. Something about the way his grandmother presented it enticed his inquisitiveness. There were copies of several large sheets of paper which bore the heading: Pension Record-National Archives, Washington, DC. He knew this was Purnell's. Below these pages rested some yellowed, soiled envelopes: the letters. One, in particular, was more frayed than the rest. The fifth one, in the bottom of the box, exhibited different handwriting than the smaller ones. He decided to save all the letters for tomorrow evening. Tonight, he'd tackle the pension record and uncover what he could about Purnell and his family. Meanwhile, Quinn glanced over page after page of the pension. He tried to skim it quickly, so later he'd study more closely the sections that detailed Purnell's service.

Quinn arranged over-sized pillows around him to be more comfortable and stacked at his feet the Civil War books he'd checked out of the library. He perused the books, especially ones with black-and-white photographs in order to visualize more clearly that era. Unhurried, he refocused attention to the pension document.

All at once, Quinn thought his imagination was playing tricks on him. Was he dreaming, or did he think he just heard Purnell say, "I'm in here—read these words more carefully, and you'll get to know me."

******

Instantly, the air in the room pulled from his body, much like being sucked into a giant vacuum. At the same time, pages held over his quilt blurred, and Quinn was conscious he was in a different reality. No longer in his room upon his bed, he now stood in Purnell's day, beside a sleeping man in a canvas tent upon a cot. The snores of other men, still asleep, surrounded him. Though Quinn didn't know how he knew, he just knew the man before him was his great-great-great-great-grandfather! For a split second, he thought he should slip out and run away. But where could he run? And what if some of the other men were startled by his movement and thought he was there to steal something? No, his only course was to wake his sleeping ancestor. Surely, his relative would allow him to explain himself. Gently Quinn nudged Purnell's shoulder. Slowly his forefather turned over on his back, yawned, stretched, and seemed unaffected or amazed by his appearance. In fact, Purnell instantly whispered to him, "Come with me."

Together they walked out the flap door of the tent, careful not to wake any of the men, soundly asleep. Very quickly they were beside some horses tethered to a hitching post already saddled, ready for them to ride. Dressed in his blue uniform, Purnell helped Quinn get onto the saddle then mounted his animal. Strangely, all these incidents appeared as if he was expected to be there. Quinn followed Purnell without question through the predawn light until they reached an open field. While he drew up beside him, Purnell pointed to an area and remarked, "A week ago this terrain was littered with more dead men and horses than you could count. As saddler of my company, the captain sent me into that chaos to remove equipage off dead beasts. All to re-outfit for our cavalry."

Quinn let his eyes sweep over terrain as the dawn light began to appear. Now he viewed clearly effects of a massive battle. Gouges in the earth's surface, along with piles of debris yet to be cleared away were evident, though any human dead were buried.

Purnell spoke again, "In your day, people will come and look at these Pennsylvania fields; some in wonder, others in horror at what happened during those three days of battle. Fathers and sons alike died, never returned to their families. All believed their cause just. Quinn, none of us know the length of our days. Learn to cherish each day as a gift and discover how to help those in need around you."

Purnell's last words were spoken so softly, Quinn had to lean forward in his saddle to hear him. But as he did so, he felt himself start to fall, and the sudden motion made Quinn jump.

The next awareness Quinn felt was finding himself on top the quilts of his bed once more.

******

The following night didn't come quickly enough for Quinn. As hard as he tried, his lack of focus in Mr. Meaker's math class earlier in the day ended in disaster when a pop quiz occurred the last fifteen minutes of the lesson. His preoccupation by what he experienced the night before kept his thoughts brooding over his encounter with Purnell and how it all had happened in the first place. Though uncertainty in his forefather's life remained, one thing Quinn did know with certainty—he'd failed the quiz.

Finally finished with homework and chores, he'd try to make sense of the events that baffled him. Quinn scoured the pension record a second time. There, he clearly saw Purnell's military service stated the years, 1863–1864, Saddler of Company G, Third Cavalry Regiment, private in rank, noted beside the official inscription of his muster date. Underneath were pages written by his widow and two companions, fellow soldiers who served alongside him during the war. In these records, Quinn read how his ancestor's demise came from an outbreak of measles, which left his wife and four children without a husband and father. Suddenly it hit him. These were his ancestors, his family too! No longer, old-fashioned names printed on a family tree. Purnell's death was listed, June 22, 1864. Eleven months after Gettysburg and just ten months before war's end. How sad it seemed he survived one of the bloodiest battles of the Civil War only to die from a disease so easily preventable today.

The longer Quinn tried to concentrate on Purnell's features in his mind, the more frustrated he became, for only a haze of a face emerged. One clear recollection kept replaying in his mind: "None of us know the length of our days. Learn to cherish each day as a gift and discover how to help those in need around you."

Abruptly, Quinn decided to alter his focus and decipher the antiquated script of William's letters. *Perhaps,* he thought, *a change in direction would enable him to see things more clearly once he returned to Purnell's documents later.*

Grandma Libby warned him there were several misspelled words in the letters, but she also said: "Try to read them as phonetically as possible to figure out their meaning." Quickly, it became evident to Quinn the four smaller letters weren't between husband and wife, but father and daughter.

> My dearist Sarah,
>
> I will try to keep yur letters safe. I read them agin and agin for they bring you befor me as if we were sitting together on the front porch of our homeplace. Tell yur ma not to worry so about me. I no she herd news of Frank's dying in the skirmish a few weeks ago but he did not sufer long. He was a good man-a good frend-but part we must in this war. Thers little time for sorow.—Even over life-long nabors. We marcht nine miles today with only one meal rachun in our bellys. We are headed into Yankee country. I dont no when I will git to rite you next. I no yur ma caint read this so tell her I love her and fondly think of her face in my dreems. Help her with all the little ones, Sarah. You are sore-prest to do all yur chores and rite these letters to, but keep up yur lerning. I love you.
>
> Papa

Quinn's concentration to understand the meaning of William's letter made him more tired than he realized. Before he read Sarah's reply, he felt his head nod from exhaustion. He was too worn out to dream tonight. Or so he thought.

As he looked down at his well-worn jeans and comfortable sweatshirt, he hadn't the strength to drag his limbs the few steps to the chest of drawers where his pajamas lay folded.

******

Momentarily, Quinn became dazed, and in that instant found himself on the very battlefield where he observed his forefather the evening before. Only now, he was directly behind Purnell, who gave him the impression he knew of Quinn's presence. With a wave of his arm, Purnell motioned Quinn to follow.

"We're headed to that dead horse over yonder. That's a McClellan saddle, an officer's. My captain wants it."

At this encounter, Quinn realized he wasn't on the battlefield the week that followed the engagement, but perhaps a day after. He picked his way through the carnage following step by step behind Purnell. Corpses lay stiff all around him, contorted and misshapen, but the odd distinction between his experience from the night before was that all these images were in gray, hazy tones—except one. His ancestor's uniform stood in stark contrast; his back, a vivid dark blue guided him onward. Strangely quiet, they maneuvered around the bodies of death. Even smell didn't assault his nostrils. Just the eerie, almost colorless landscape of human and horse flesh scattered everywhere. Quinn felt he was part of a Matthew Brady photograph, literally on a walk inside one. He wondered how out of place he must look in this scene: a twelve-year-old boy from the twenty-first century, in jeans, with a school logo emblazoned across his shirt. Despite this, Purnell still treated him as normal—just normal.

At last, they reached the dead horse. While Purnell began to recover the saddle, they both turned to an unanticipated cry: "Wa-ter, w-w-w-ater!" Quinn's eyes followed the sound with a zoom-in quality. A haggard face that lay among the mass of gray came distinctly into focus. Hair disheveled and matted, draped slightly over the man's shoulders. A wound, just under his right collarbone, revealed stark color to the gray of his uniform: deep burgundy. The man's pain was evident, but his thirst was sheer agony. Purnell carried a canteen toward the tormented soldier and supported his head. Quinn stood back and surveyed the surreal circumstances as they played out. The wounded soldier seemed unaffected that someone so out of place as he, viewed this scene so openly.

With a trembling hand, the injured soldier reached into his breast pocket and removed some folded paper. He spoke to Purnell in broken sobs, "M-m-m-my daughter. Would you write her, and tell her you saw me? Tell her, tell her I promise I'll write as soon as I'm strong enough, but in case, soldier, will you…just tell her I'll do my best to come home. Her name is Sarah, Sarah Elizabeth Killingsworth, Pittsboro, Mississippi."

Purnell answered back kindly, "Well, what do you know? I have a daughter named Sarah Elizabeth too! Sarah.... Elizabeth...Chance. And yes soldier, I'll be happy to write your daughter for you."

At that very moment, Quinn felt his hand push aside some papers and the scene was gone. When he sat up, he saw the pages of William's letters scattered across his bed.

******

Though events kept Quinn from reading the balance of the letters over the next few days, he was confident he'd discover answers to loose ends once he finished them.

Tuesday evening kept him busy with his team's weekly soccer game. Forced to suffer consequences, Quinn spent the game sidelined; the result of his plummeting math grade. Determined to study and bring it up, he produced a scheduled plan to his parents and soccer coach to achieve his goal. Under normal circumstances, the sport required his utmost focus but sidelined as he was, Quinn found the game's excitement paled in comparison to the recent adventures with his ancestors. How he'd explain all this to Grandma Libby was a mystery to him. Could he tell her? For all he knew, these adventures had been a boy's vivid imagination gone awry. Still, he cautioned himself, he only experienced these dreams or visions in his room, just before bedtime. He wondered if a different setting would produce a different outcome.

It was Thursday before another opportunity permitted him a chance to view the documents again. Quinn deliberately planned to choose the right location in order to have some privacy. Naturally, the only logical place to achieve fewer distractions was the attic. In summer, the heat was intolerable, but this was October, and he realized he'd be comfortable in such seclusion. Upon entering, he cracked open an attic window just enough to freshen the air. Then Quinn arranged large boxes to make a table, and, on top, placed the documents his grandmother gave him. Along with a flashlight, he'd brought his journal, pencil, and some snacks. He'd persevere until dinnertime at least. Up here, he knew he'd constantly be on guard for attic spiders. Surely, the increasing wariness would lessen any possibility his imagination might play tricks on him.

As Quinn read the second letter, Sarah's response to her father's, nothing struck him as out of the ordinary. She merely spoke of farm life and friendly neighbors. Her words attempted to soothe her father's distress by explaining how they managed sufficiently in his absence.

It was the third letter from William that quickened Quinn's pulse so peculiarly.

> July 10, 1863
> Dearist Sarah,
>
> I cannot explane to you in words what has hapened here since I last rote. Even if I coud, it woud only worry you and yur dear ma to keenly. Sufice it to say,

our compne took a grate defeet in batle and I have lost many a dear comrade. Thoh woonded and fallen, I thawt thirst and exhouschun woud prevent me from leavin this place alive, when the act of one kind man, a soljer undr the enemes baner, savd my life. My dearist, when the batle was over and dun, even the color of a mans unaform made no difrince. We wer all men callin out to our God for help, and my help came from a compashunate man. I gave him yur name and addres in kase I coud not rite you. He told me he had a dauter named Sarah Elizabeth as well. I have not seen him sinse, but I shall nevr forget his kindness. Sarah, I am redy to put this war behind me and come home. My woonds to the sholder are mendin and we who are prisonrs will soon be taken to a place further north called Pea Patch I-land. Fort Deleware, I'm told. Tis a long way from my dearist famly. As soon as I am able I will rite agin. But I dont no when pen and paper will be avalabel to me. Perheps not for a very long time. Never lose hart dear ones. I have kept yur letters near me all these many miles I have marcht. They bring me such comfert and hope. Pray for me Sarah and tell yur ma how much I love her.

Love,
Papa

Stunned by how closely events in William's letter matched the recent experience with his forefathers, Quinn picked up the fourth letter and read:

September 9, 1863
Oh my Papa,

Ma and I shed many a tear over your last letter. We've read it a thousand times and still cry at each reading. To know you were so badly hurt and left uncared for til that good Samartin came to your rescue. The Lord truly sent him. I smiled when you said his girl was given the same name as mine. I wonder what she's like and how old she must be? Papa, I don't know if you'll get this letter. We asked the postmaster how to send it to the prison named Fort Delaware. He told us it should get to you, but they may read the letter before you do. We pray for you always and long for you to be home. If you're weak and tired, don't worry, we can make a living working our land together. The girls and John are all getting stronger and more help to me and ma every day. Ma says she loves you and will keep your place set at the table ready, should you surprise us soon and come home.

Your devoted daughter,
Sarah E.

As Quinn finished reading the letter, a question hit him: "How could these father-daughter communications end up in the possession of his grandmother?" He'd need to ask her on Saturday.

Quinn inspected the envelopes painstakingly and realized they weren't the original ones at all; though very old, they didn't have addresses labeled on them. The two envelopes with Sarah's letters inside were in a simple script: To Wm J. Killingsworth, From Sarah Elizabeth Killingsworth. Further, he examined the penmanship of Sarah's handwriting to the envelopes and saw they were different. The same was true for the handwriting on William's letters.

At some point over the years, whether, from too much handling or fragility, the envelopes were replaced by newer ones he surmised. Briefly, Quinn closed his eyes and massaged his temples to relax. He looked up again and peered off into a dark corner of the attic. All questions primarily formulated into one: "How did two soldiers, absolute strangers to one another, possibly become his forefathers?" He'd have to study the family tree at his grandma's house once he got there. The longer he stared into the corner, however, the deeper and darker it became. Immediately, he was walking through a long, shadowy tunnel.

******

"I'm over here," a voice faintly whispered as Quinn strained to hear it.

The next thing he knew he was thrust beside his ancestor, Purnell, again.

Time had no meaning nor seemed confined by its usual constraints whenever Quinn found himself in these circumstances. What appeared to happen in moments may have taken hours in Quinn's world. *But now was not the time to sort it all out,* he thought. *Just experience it and try to make sense of it all later.*

The man he knew who lay before him on a cot held little resemblance to the figure he recalled from earlier encounters. If it weren't for the familiar voice, he'd perhaps have second-guessed that here lay, Private Purnell Chance, of the US Cavalry.

Covered in woolen blankets and evidently chilled, Purnell quivered his shoulders and struggled to move the covers more tightly around him. His face, so fevered, and his dark hair combed back, seemed wet as if he'd just come from a bath. Moreover, Purnell was a mere shell of the ancestor he last saw.

What happened to him? Quinn bemused. Then suddenly, he remembered the words in the pension document.

Oh no! I have to find someone to help; to save him!

Once again, Purnell spoke, "Over here! O-o-over here!"

Quinn started to bolt closer when he was aware of another person beside him Purnell addressed. Now, Quinn wondered if his forefather even discerned his presence. Just then, the figure rushed to Purnell's side to attend him. He wanted to say something, but his voice froze as he watched the middle-aged man cared for Purnell. *He must be a military doctor,* Quinn thought. *He wears no coat, and his shirt sleeves are pulled to his elbows. His trousers, tucked in shiny boots, appear soldierly.*

Quinn slowly walked around the foot of the cot to motion he was there to help. Then he heard, ever so quietly, Purnell say, "Doctor, will you mail the letter in my pocket to my daughter, Sarah? I need to tell her something."

The physician patted his arm and responded, "Of course, Private. I'll be happy to do that for you."

At that moment, Purnell's eyes met Quinn's. His ancestor nodded and smiled as if to say, good-bye.

The next instant, Quinn was aware of his attic surroundings once more.

******

"Please pass your papers forward and turn in your books to page 139," said Mr. Meaker.

Though Quinn went through his responsibilities like any other school day, he carried his experience from the night before like a heavy burden. Despite learning early on that Purnell died of measles, Quinn was still shocked. Besides that, the advanced warning Grandma Libby conveyed hadn't prepared him for the impact this latest vision had given him.

"Quinn, what are the key words in this passage that might signal the main character's problem?" Mr. Meaker asked.

Oh no, he thought, *caught off guard again!*

Later that evening, Quinn held the final letter in his hand and wondered what would be in store for him. He decided to stay in his room since he knew no matter where he studied, the documents continued to come alive. Tomorrow, he'd meet with his grandma and state the facts he'd learned. That's all; he promised himself.

Now he focused on the fifth letter. The one all along delegated to the bottom of the box. He realized it was Purnell's missive, although the outside cover only bore the name, Sarah.

As he took a deep breath, his hand tremored. Slowly, he opened it and read:

> June 12, 1864
> Dear Sarah,
>
> My darling girl, I know you find it unusual for me to write you and not your dear mother, but I have something only you can do for me. I made a promise to a soldier some time ago, a wounded soldier, at Gettysburg. He gave me a special request. He wanted me to write his daughter and let her know he was wounded but hoped, by war's end, to come home. That soldier was not Union but Confederate. He lay severely injured for several hours after the battle. On my way through the littered battlefield, I heard his cry for help. I couldn't turn him away. Later I was told the captured prisoners, healthy and wounded alike, were taken to Fort Delaware, about six thousand of them. I hope he made it. I don't know if he did. I wasn't able to find him again. Regretfully, I never fulfilled the promise I made to him, so I'm asking you. He told me he also had a daughter

> named Sarah Elizabeth. I think it would mean more if she received the letter from someone who shares her name. Post it to, Sarah Elizabeth Killingsworth, Pittsboro, Mississippi. Let her know her father was alive after the battle and spoke lovingly of her. Tell your mother I'll write her soon. I've taken ill this past week, and a fever has me confined to my cot. Give my love to the boys and Susan, and always remember what I told you the day I left.
>
> Love,
> Papa

Quinn marveled how he could visualize the scene so clearly after reading the final letter. Then he recalled what his grandma told him: "We're all given a window of time." The documents he studied this past week allowed him to open that window on Purnell and William's day. Now, he couldn't help but wonder what evidence he'd leave behind for his descendants to discover, someday in the future.

The gravel road to his grandparent's home jostled Quinn in his seat from twists and turns his mother's car took while questions pitched around his head. Somehow, he realized, Grandma Libby held the key unlocking those issues. Quinn understood she knew all along where his quests would lead him. Now that day was here. At last, he'd learn just how it all unfolded for Purnell and William, as well as when the two families became connected.

Purnell Chance
Sarah E Chance,

Once inside his grandma's kitchen smells greeted him from a corner wood stove mixed with the aroma of orange, spiced tea.

"Quinn, I can't wait to hear what you've learned! While the cookies are baking, why don't you go into my office and look at the family tree I framed? It's on the wall."

Quinn found the family tree, finished, framed in a predominating place. Quickly, he located Purnell and William's names but concentrated more carefully on the generations that joined surnames. *Ah! I can't believe I didn't pay more attention to this before! Sarah Elizabeth Chance married a Cummings and had a boy named George. Sarah Elizabeth Killingsworth married a Davis and had a girl named Clara. George and Clara Cummings are my grandmother's grandparents! That makes Purnell and William her great-great-grandfathers, just as she told me. But how did George and Clara meet?*

Quinn brought his notes to the kitchen table, along with documents and Civil War books from the library.

"I see you've developed some good historian techniques with your resources and journal of notes," his grandma stated while she thumbed through pages.

"Grandma Libby, I experienced more history than I thought possible," Quinn countered back, wondering if she understood his hint.

"Why don't you tell me what you've uncovered about Purnell and William, and then I'll try to fill in any gaps," she said.

Quinn read aloud from his journal how he began with the pension document. As more details spilled out, he grew more excited. His grandma picked up on his eagerness and interrupted, "You know, Quinn. You have an inquisitive gift. As you research, dig deeper into historical facts that you'll find during your investigations. Then more light will be shed on what could have happened while they lived. Of course, the more primary documents you discover, the better you'll understand what life might have been like for them. Now, I see you want to know from here in your notes how William passed away. Several years ago, I decided to look into my grandmother's history and confirm what she told me about her grandfather, William, a Mississippi Confederate, who'd fought at Gettysburg. When I researched further, I discovered documents that proved she was correct and learned he died in February of 1864 while a prisoner at Fort Delaware. His body was buried on the Jersey shore of the fort, never to be joined with his family again."

With heartache, Quinn no longer was amazed someone that far removed by generations triggered such emotion.

"Let's see," said his grandma, as she came to the end of his journal. "You ask how we descended from these two very different gentlemen, and just how the two families joined when one fought for the north, and the other, the south? Now that, I can answer! But first, let's enjoy a plate of warm cookies and hot tea."

Later, after Quinn and Grandma Libby carried their empty plates and cups to the kitchen sink, they cleaned off the table and sat down comfortably to talk.

"Grandson, if I told you all I learned from Purnell and William without giving you the opportunity to dig up facts yourself, their lives wouldn't have meant as much to you, little more than just unusual names on a page.

Quinn nodded in agreement.

"When I was a small girl my grandmother gave me this box with the skeleton key. Inside it was an old doll, some embroidered pillowcases, a thimble, and these five letters. She let me play with the doll, and the other items I placed on top of the documents you now hold. I added the pension document of Purnell years ago after I ordered it from Washington, DC. You see, Quinn, the rest of the story cannot be told through investigation or research, but by oral tradition. You're hearing it from your grandmother, who heard it from her grandmother, about her grandfather."

She took his hand in hers and continued, "Quinn, a part of them is in you. But ultimately, you had to make the decision whether or not to track down through research what you could to find out about them. I like the fact that you stuck with it and didn't quit over questions that remained. Now as you're aware; the four smaller letters were between William and his daughter, Sarah. My grandmother Clara told me the story of how those letters came to her this way."

At that very moment, the phone rang, and Quinn's grandma motioned him to wait.

Several minutes later, Quinn and his grandma sat relaxed in chairs around the kitchen table with cups of hot tea. "Remember, William died in prison camp, but Purnell wasn't aware of that when he wrote his daughter. My grandmother explained the events like this: her mother, Sarah Killingsworth was a teenager by the end of the Civil War when a letter from Indiana arrived at her home in Mississippi. The moment Sarah Elizabeth Killingsworth saw the name, Sarah Elizabeth Chance, on the return address, she remembered what her father had told her in his last letter. Curious, she opened the letter and read what you already know was written. You see, all the letters she'd written her father as well as his personal articles came back to the Killingsworth family from the prison in late March of 1864, including a note stating her father's death. The only things my grandmother gave me, however, were four letters, plus the fifth one from Purnell."

Quinn could bear it no longer, "So how did an Indiana family get together with a Mississippi family?"

Patting his arm, she said, "My grandmother Clara told me a bond grew between the two Sarahs'. One letter that began their correspondence turned into many, all the way to adulthood. What happened to those series of letters, I don't know, but she found out an important move took place. Her Mississippi family purchased inexpensive farmland in Arkansas and months later the Chances paid them a visit. By that time, the Mississippi Sarah, now a Davis, had a beautiful daughter name Clara. The Indiana Sarah, a Cummings, had a handsome son named George. As you must have guessed, the Indiana family decided to remain in Arkansas and naturally, both Sarahs' ended up as dear friends for the remainder of their lives. More unusual, however, they became in-laws, since George and Clara fell in love and married."

Quinn had one lingering question not yet resolved. He asked, "So how did Purnell's letter come into your collection?"

Grandma Libby answered, "One day, equally as curious about my Indiana Sarah, I asked grandfather George to tell me about his mother: Sarah Elizabeth Chance. He relayed to me how his parents moved south but not long after, his mother became ill with tuberculosis. In her final days, she wanted to give him Purnell's letter that started the two Sarahs' friendship. On her deathbed, George felt compelled to ask her, 'In the letter your papa wrote, he asked you to always remember what he told you the day he left for war. Do you remember what he said?"

She answered him, "Of course, how could I ever forget that! My papa said, 'Sarah, none of us know the length of our days. Learn to cherish each day as a gift and discover how to help those in need around you.'"

Quinn smiled and knew from that moment on, Purnell's words would be carried in his heart, forever.

******

The characters and events in this story are based on actual ancestors of the author although the correct sequence of generations and particular events were changed.

George and Clara Cummings were the author's grandparents. However, the two Sarahs' were grandmothers rather than mothers of the couple.

William Killingsworth served as a corporal in the Forty-Second Mississippi Infantry and suffered an injury at Gettysburg. He later died while captive, as the story portrayed, at Fort Delaware, Pea Patch Island.

Purnell Chance was a private and Saddler for the Third Regiment, United States Cavalry, but didn't fight at Gettysburg. He died in a military hospital at Little Rock, Arkansas, June 1864. Purnell is buried at the National Cemetery in Little Rock, Arkansas.

In truth, both men had daughters named Sarah Elizabeth; however, the Sarahs' never met one another.

Purnell's thirty-page pension document from the National Archives offered valuable information about his service and family for this story.

The letters between both men and their daughters are fictional.

Peter's Discovery

May 26, 2014

GRANDMA LIBBY PEERED over Peter's shoulder as he sketched a horse bounding a split-rail fence. "Why, your dad loved to draw horses too. I see you have his talent for it. Now where do you imagine your horse is off to?"

"What do you mean, Grandma?" he asked.

"Well, you have him jumping a fence. Do you think he's in a race to be in such a hurry?"

Peter scanned his artwork more closely. "Yes, and my horse is in the lead. Perhaps it's even a hunt."

"I like that," Grandma Libby confirmed. "Come here a moment, sweetheart," she said while she motioned him to follow her into another room. There she opened a dresser drawer full of an assortment of things: school ribbons, awards, graded homework papers, and last, a variety of artwork. As she paged the latter, she spotted what she sought. "Here it is."

Grandma Libby continued, "This was your dad's picture that looks similar to your own. See, his horse was on a race and jumped a fence as well.

Peter said, "Only there's a saddle on him, without a rider. I wonder why Dad drew his that way?"

"Oh he probably portrayed him like that after I told him the story about the general," Grandma Libby answered.

"The general?" Peter queried. "What story are you talking about?"

"Well," she said. "Let me read you the story I wrote for your dad a long time ago..." Sometime in the year 1746, the youngest son of George and Margaret Davidson was born in Pennsylvania. His name was William Lee, and as a young boy he and his family joined a wagon train of settlers to claim land by squatter rights in North Carolina. In his youth, William became an expert marksman while he hunted through forests with his musket. William's early years imparted him with knowledge of meadows, creeks, and woods that made up a frontier existence. One particular day, he set off to bag meat for a celebratory meal, when, to the delight of his family he triumphantly arrived home holding high, five wild turkeys. Though he lived an idyllic existence for a pioneer boy, William's humble emergence onto life's stage did not come without sacrifice. As a teenager, he learned how joy and sorrow entwine together like strands of a rope. In the year 1760, his parents died. As a result, he was left in the care of an older cousin named George, like his father, where William performed the same duties with much the same resourcefulness he had for his own family. Consequently, William plunged into adulthood with experiences that framed his character like a portrait, once unveiled, rendering him a future soldier of distinguished reputation and honor. In his twenty-first year, William's cousin, eighteen years older than he, beseeched him one day with these words: "William, come; walk with me to the stables. I have something I want to show you." In a leisurely manner, George escorted him and spoke, "You've worked hard these seven years living with our family. Catherine and I know you and Mary will make an excellent family of your own. I've witnessed your growth from a boy to a man while you labored here on the farm. Not once did you complain to till my soil, clean the stable yard, or split wood for the fire." George unlatched the gate to the stable grounds and continued, "Reports have returned favorable of our spring expeditions with the governor's guard into Cherokee country. I've heard rumors the governor was impressed by the men of Rowan and the closeness of their firing."(1)[i] At this, George squeezed William's shoulder to confirm his praise.

"I observed you, William, while you maneuvered your horse during an assault on a borrowed saddle through rugged terrain, taking care of your animal at the end of a ride, diligent to comb his dampened coat; then prize another man's saddle as if it were your own. I saw you made certain to keep it dry and off the ground every evening. That's why I want you to have this." At that moment, George opened the door of his workshop attached to the Davidson stable yard. Predominately in the center of the room sat a new leather saddle with bridle—exquisite in form and feature.

All William managed to say, barely above a whisper was, "Cousin." He was so overwhelmed with gratitude for the man who took him in as a thirteen-year-old orphan and gifted him in such a manner. Still stunned, but not wanting to appear ungracious, he at last found his voice.

"George, it's…magnificent!" William ran his hands across the leather, finely tooled to perfection. "I'll treasure it always!"

William wasn't ignorant about the labor such a gift entailed. He'd watched and assisted his cousin, George Davidson, local tanner, currier, and saddler; repair, as well as design and form leather into saddles for residents of their community. George, known for his *good hand* tanning the finest leather hides into a product his customers thought matchless, perfected his craft over the years. William admired George's skill, and knew he'd made this saddle from hog skin for better gripping. However, it was George's *finish work* that reflected the pride of his trade. William traced his finger around its intricate stitching. No other gift than George's held more meaning to the young lieutenant on the eve of his wedding day. Such a saddle would have cost William four months' wages.

Several years later
December 17, 1780

Now a brigadier general, William Lee Davidson finished the draft of his Last Will and Testament in front of his three friends and neighbors, who scribed their names as his witnesses. As a Continental officer, the Revolutionary War had taken William through the Battle of Germantown, the winter encampment of Washington's army in Valley Forge, and later engagements where he rose through the ranks. Eventually, he became a militia commander as well. It was during this period in his military career William adeptly recruited his countrymen to fight, when pay was short and separation from families, challenging. Esteemed for bravery by his militia, they honored their local legend. But in the end, it was his valor that brought him to an untimely death.

As a soldier, he understood the disastrous risk to leave loved ones behind without proper instructions for their future. Thus, William desired his will to reflect careful and considerate directives for his wife and children.

It read: "I give and recommend my soul unto the hands of Almighty God that gave it, and my body, I recommend to the earth, to be buried in a decent and Christian manner." Yet the next portion phrased a true soldier's heart: "I do give and bequeath unto my well-beloved wife, Mary Davidson, one blooded sorrel mare together with a saddle and bridle—besides her thirds, and likewise the use of the plantation on which I now live; until my son, George, comes of age, for which she is to take proper care of the children and give them proper learning or as much learning as she may judge necessary."(2)[ii]

After so many close calls in battle, it was not unusual for a soldier to so prepare his estate should he fall. And one day soon after, William would seriously miscalculate his enemy.

January 29, 1781

Vexed by accounts of *justice* poured out on fellow Loyalist to the British, the Tories of North Carolina surged to help England's campaign.

The British commander, Lord Cornwallis, slowly guided his army toward the region to confound his enemy about where he'd cross the Catawba River.

Brigadier General Davidson spent a night at the plantation of his relative, Major John Davidson, near Tool's Ford. The next day, he rose early to dictate orders of his command when his beloved horse appeared lame, and he was forced to borrow one of Major John's. With close to five hundred men at his disposal, he placed them at Beatties Ford to await further orders. Meanwhile, a council of war was called for their highest-ranking officers, which included General Nathaniel Greene. Realizing the British had superior numbers of troops, General Greene and the other commanders agreed to travel ahead to get closer to the main army while Davidson and his soldiers attempted to slow the British attack and make a quick getaway once the onslaught began. On the eve of February 1st, Davidson moved to Cowan's Ford along the river where two existed: a horse ford and a wagon ford. He believed the British would cross the shallower horse ford due to the recent heavy rains. However, he left a light guard behind on the more treacherous wagon ford. It was his presumption Cornwallis would wait until daylight to cross. Ultimately, William sat down at his camp to rest. Some time later, back at the wagon ford, a whistling sound was heard on the other side of the river. It was answered: likely an enemy signal. In the wee hours, splashing awoke the guards from their slumber and they cried, "The enemy, the enemy!" Quickly, they fired their guns to alarm the rest of the ranks. On hearing shots in the distance, General Davidson mounted his horse with his cavalry officer behind him and rushed half a mile toward the action. The general immediately ordered the cavalry to rush and protect the rear, while he and two other officers rode in front toward the river where danger was imminent. Davidson and his next in command, charged their horses down the embankment, unaware the enemy was already across to meet them.

At that instant, a gun fired.

Before he raised a weapon in response, General Davidson fell from his horse. In the mayhem, his steed fled back to the safety of his stable, carrying away, the general's beloved saddle.

But where was the general?

He lay dead beside the bank of the Catawba River with the gun of his Tory assassin still smoking.

Years later, locals continued to shed tears when they spoke of the day the general died.

Memorial Day, 2014

As Grandma Libby closed her eyes and sighed, Peter asked, "Grandma, may I have dad's sketch of the general's horse?"

"Of course, dear, of course…I can't think of anyone else I'd rather give it to," she replied.

******

I dedicate this story to all the men in my family who served their country in the military, starting with my son Richard, all the way back to a Revolutionary patriot and fifth great-grandfather, Brigadier General William Lee Davidson.

Rosalie's Discovery

August 5, 1929
5:30 a.m.

THE WHITE LEGHORN rallied Civility out of her dreams while the day's first light streamed through the bedroom window. Whistles blared and diminished as the nearby Cotton Belt rail called to reverie any lingering dreamer. Despite the early hour, an onerous humidity clung to the air. Sluggish from the August heat, Civility deliberately reflected on her lifelong custom: arise first and make the daily bread.

Civility Stewart was a born bread maker. One day, her mother found her playing with the dough after she'd had rescued a stray mule from an opened gate. The truth was, her mother taught Civility as a child long before the Civil War to push and breathe; push and breathe, all in a steady rhythm that worked the dough to perfection. But what may have started as play later became a chore, which served her well among kin and stranger. This day, however, Civility remained in bed as if snared by a weight of wet blankets. Her seventy-nine years maintained the bread-making custom so rigid she lay there bewildered by her sudden change of habit. For despite Civility's length in years, nothing seemed to designate she was elderly. Her grandmotherly role began late when compared to her peers. At sixty-five, Civility's only grandchild was born. Then tragically, only three years passed when she faced the loss of her daughter Ruthie from the flu epidemic of 1918. Suddenly, Civility's role turned to mother once again.

Despite everything, she never collapsed under the pressure. And when asked, Civility confessed her graduation into womanhood as being, April 1864.

Swayed to remain in bed and pamper herself with memories, she allowed her thoughts to journey like a rare morning breeze that faintly caresses, yet rides on into the depths of mind and soul.

Civility sighed and remembered…

April 30, 1864

Papa was a country doctor, farmer, and philosopher all rolled into one. His talents were never so proven though as they were after the Battle of Jenkins Ferry. Mama wanted me taken to my uncle's farm as soon as she heard the approaching march of troops and wagons that late April 1864, but rain which began steadily turned into deluge, keeping me home. I remember Papa said I was safer at home than stuck axle-deep in clay and soaked from head to toe in an opened wagon.

The troops marched roughly half a mile from our place. Large post oaks that I climbed on dry spring days surrounded it. If the weather'd been different that day, I'd have seen clouds of smoke from the battle. But the steady downpour made it impossible.

Our single-story home supported a gabled roof with a lone window in the attic. As a child, Mama let me make use of this cramped space for a playroom when it was either dead winter or sultry heat in summer. Open porches enclosed three sides of the house. An extended porch-like hallway connected Papa's workroom facing north, extending to the kitchen along the rear.

Papa had graduated from a medical school in Philadelphia and rode his Arabian horse, Hercules, to southern Arkansas to begin his career. On that April day, however, Papa instructed Mama and me how we'd be most helpful. He sent Mama through the house pulling old quilts and linen out of storage trunks; making bandages as well as getting the house and barn ready to become hospitals. My task was to collect rainwater in buckets as it dripped from the porch roof and pour into empty barrels Papa had moved along the breezeway. With all preparations complete, he told Mama and I to sleep as much as possible though the fighting in the near distance sounded intense. Like thunder, rumbling canons exploded both earth and flesh alike. Rifles answered back as though soldiers were right outside the house, on target practice in the walnut grove between our place and the Saline. Papa told the scout hours before he'd have the place transformed into a hospital by the time they needed it.

At some point, I must have fallen into a deep sleep, because the next thing I remembered, stood a group of strange men; some carried while others hobbled in, but all suffered from various injuries. The sight of blood had never scared me. Papa worked that out of me long before when I'd helped him with wounded farm animals that needed his surgical skills. I was always strangely fascinated by his keen ability to know just where to cut, what to remove, and how to sew it all back together using the same precision Mama did piecing her quilts. What jarred me into reality that day wasn't the blood or severity of the soldier's wounds, but the mud. The god-awful, smelly mud mixed with near death. Every soldier, without exception, looked as if he'd been rolling in it. Later, as the sun broke through the clouds, it created the distinct odor of baked mud pies mixed with sweat and gore.

Right away, men poured into the front parlor. Orders came to push furniture next to walls so patients might sit or lie down until it was their turn. I was instantly called to action—all fourteen years of me.

Needing to separate the soldiers by the severity of injuries, Papa allocated the least hurt to the house where Mama and a handful of neighbor women patched them up. He staged himself in the barn, where wooden floors created a hollow echo as men's boots wore paths back and forth between a makeshift operating table and door. Rays of sunlight poured through cracks in the barn's boarded walls. Kerosene lanterns hung, where the open door's light failed to reach. Agonized moans from the wounded kept Lizzie and Delcey, servant women from a nearby neighbor, employed pacifying those ready for surgery or those who'd just returned.

I began as Papa's runner and messenger between the house and barn, but as the long day wore into evening, Papa realized my help by his side would be more advantageous. By the time Mama understood my position, the necessity of my needed skills had outweighed any argument against it. There was little time for prolonged conversation that day or into the night. Each person found a role to perform and carried it out as best he could, regardless of prior knowledge or experience.

The dawn of May 1st pierced its light through the barn's loft window. Whispered quiet cloaked the area as if all the living were in prayer. Occasional groans from soldiers in pain drifted out my mind. It was then I looked down for the first time. The barn's wood floor was a patchwork of red and gray in places so slick with blood, Delcey took a handful of straw to spread over its slipperiness. Papa detected my exhaustion and urged me back to the house for some rest.

As I stepped onto the front porch, I noticed a soldier by the door on an improvised cot closest to the entry. The wounds on his face and neck were cleaned to dress his battle scars, but mud and dirty water so caked his uniform that I realized he must have been one pulled from the riverbank. When I walked passed him, he reached out his arm and yanked my skirt toward him.

"What is it, sir?" I asked.

"May I have a drink from that barrel over there? I've longed for refreshment all night."

"Surely, sir," I said.

As I handed him a dipper full of water, I looked more closely at his uniform and realized a trace of blue beneath the dirt and mud. He observed my scrutiny and uttered, "Thank you for the water. I'm obliged your kindness, and, yes, I'm a long way from home."

"Where's your home?" I asked.

"Iowa," he answered.

I smiled back about to leave when he tugged my skirt once more.

"Young lady, if you'd do one favor for me I'd be most beholden," he said.

"Certainly, sir," I confirmed, "if it's within my power to do so."

"Would you cut a curl from my hair and place it in a letter to my wife? It's been over a month since I wrote her. I don't believe I'll make it home," the soldier said.

I thought his wound wasn't severe enough for such a verdict; however, to pacify him, I answered, "Certainly, sir, I'll return shortly with a pair of scissors and some writing tools and stationary." Once I reappeared, I sat beside him as he dictated touching words to his wife. Then I took a lock of hair, unsullied by mud, cut it, and held it up for his inspection. "Will this do?"

"Yes," he reciprocated with a warm smile.

I walked away, but said over my shoulder, "I'll mail it as soon as time permits." I concealed the letter for safekeeping behind a loose chimney brick in our parlor fireplace. It was days, of course, before I posted the soldier's letter. I only prayed he was wrong in his prophecy though I didn't indicate his foreboding in the letter to his wife.

Duties and errands kept me so busy I never found out when or where that soldier was returned to the care of his army, or as a prisoner to ours. Of course, it was later in life before I realized the impact those days had on me. They always climbed to the surface when I pushed my palm into soft, pliable dough for kneading. Those memories rose like the yeast inflating my bread, expanding my experiences into lifelong lessons worthy of remembrance.

August 5, 1929
6:00 a.m.

In the stillness, another recollection surfaced as Civility struggled to carry out her morning duty. *Oh, what would it hurt*, she thought, *it's still an hour before I need to wake up Rosalie. I'll just savor this moment and recall another special day. It can't take more than a few minutes to relax here and remember, again.*

One month earlier
July 4, 1929

The drive to my old homeplace took an hour through graveled roads and low creek water bridges. While we rode along, Rosalie listened intently to my story of that April day so long ago when I served as a nurse to Papa. At last, we reached the structure, now mostly gray, with flecks of white paint behind a lone giant, post oak in the front yard.

"May I go inside, Grandma? I want to see your parlor?" she asked.

Hesitant, I said, "Do be careful. There may be rotten boards. I don't want you to fall through! Step lightly."

While I waited beside the car, I was lost in recollections of so many happy and sad times when Rosalie exclaimed, "Grandma, I've found it!" She ran to me with a large object in her hand. "It's your brick from the parlor fireplace. It was loose, just as you said. Your Papa didn't repair the chimney, even after the war?"

"Well, of all things! It truly is my brick. I can tell because it's chipped precisely in the place I recall. And no, Papa never repaired it because he knew I'd tuck trinkets there."

"May I have the brick, Grandma, for a keepsake?" Rosalie asked.

"I don't see why not. This place will be gone soon, like the barn before it. None of the family that's left wants to live here anymore."

August 5, 1929
7:00a.m.

Civility was up half an hour making bread, relishing Rosalie's happy day the month before. Though her home didn't accommodate a fireplace, her granddaughter found a corner cabinet where she placed the brick to hide what she valued. *Before too many years, Rosalie will have a place of her own to store it,* Civility thought.

As she covered the dough in a bowl to rise, Civility smiled over the memories. It was time for Rosalie to wake up and gather morning eggs from the hen house. But when Civility opened the door, her joy turned to somber dismay. Rosalie's agony was evident; her body looked bathed with fever. Unable to speak above a whisper, Rosalie couldn't have called for help, nor have walked to the washroom in her weakened state.

Once again, Civility's nursing skills were summoned into action.

After cleaning Rosalie with cool washcloths, she changed her bedding and attire. At last, Civility hurried to telephone the doctor. His evaluation an hour later was thorough, but his prognosis grim.

"She's terribly ill, Civility. She kept telling me her neck was hurting. I don't want to alarm you, but it might be spinal meningitis. There was a local girl her age that died of it a couple of weeks ago. Was she around Mary Stillwell?" he asked.

"Why yes!" Civility answered in alarm. "I hadn't heard she died of meningitis."

"Well, do what you can to keep her comfortable. She'll alternate between high fever, then chills. She might improve if we've caught it early enough."

Civility didn't know where the strength came from, but she managed to get through the day caring for Rosalie with determined perseverance. At last toward evening, Rosalie took hold of her grandmother's apron she'd worn since the morning bread making. Softly, she requested, "Grandma, would you cut a curl from my hair?"

Civility gasped, "Rosalie, why are you asking me that?"

"In case I don't make it, Grandma, please? I want it to go with my other treasures behind the brick. There's no one else who loves me as much as you. I know you'd take it out and look at it whenever you wanted to remember me.

"Now, Rosalie, you're going to pull through and grow into a fine young lady. Don't talk like that. I wish I'd never told you that old story!" Civility said.

"No, Grandma, don't you see why your story is so special to me? It's important to know you'll have a part of me to touch and remember."

Reluctantly, Civility took her scissors and cut an auburn lock from Rosalie's braid. As she placed it into a small envelope for safe-keeping behind the brick, her grandmother smiled at her, and Rosalie fell soundly asleep.

One year later

Civility beamed at her granddaughter across the room while she chatted with a friend. Surprised by her granddaughter's candid insistence a year earlier to cut a curl for a keepsake memory, she was amazed Rosalie fought so hard to stay alive. Soon after recovery, Rosalie remarked one day, "Grandma, when I was ill, in and out of fever, I realized I was the same age as you when you helped your Papa care for all those injured soldiers during the war. I couldn't let go of that thought, and indeed, I understood you needed me more now. So I prayed to the Lord, if it be His will, please let me live, so I could take care of you."

******

I grew up listening to stories my grandmother told me of her grandmother who lived in southern Arkansas during the Civil War. Many times she used to take me on drives around the countryside while she pointed out homesteads of her ancestors. On one occasion, she came to her great-great-uncle's home that served as a Civil War hospital, along with the barn after the Battle of Marks's Mill. As a little girl in the early 1900s, my grandmother recalled playing in the old barn with her cousins and bloodstains, still visible, were on the barn's wooden floor. On the day of my visit, the barn was long gone, but the house, though dilapidated, begged me to enter. Once inside the parlor, I walked over to the old brick fireplace and noticed a loose brick. I wriggled it free. Years later, that brick became the inspiration for this story. In 'Rosalie's Discovery,' I moved the family to experience the Jenkins Ferry Battle instead.

Etta's Discovery

August 15, 1841

"Mr. Shortridge, you said your wife enjoys needlework?"

"Oh yes, she always carries her needle and thread with her at home."

"How about a lovely sterling thimble for her birthday," the clerk said. "If you'll follow me this way, we have some excellent selections behind that counter. I'm certain you'll find one suitable for her."

William Shortridge walked behind the clerk with a slight limp to his gait from the wounds he'd received years before during the War of 1812. His boots tapped a powerful rhythm as he crossed the plank floor, and his suit, well-worn, slightly out of season, conveyed this his one and only. William's round, gray-bearded face radiated excitement over the surprise he had in store for Elizabeth. It only took moments before he found one he thought exceptional, detailing intricate scrollwork around its edge.

"You know, Mr. Shortridge, while you run other errands in Owensboro, why don't you leave your gift with Mr. Milroy, the jeweler next door, to engrave your wife's initials on it? Just think how personal an engraved thimble would be for her," the clerk added.

Hours later, William Shortridge stopped his horse. The fingers on his hand tingled, and he wondered if he ought to stop and stretch his legs before he continued the ride home.

He'd left Owensboro with a supply of nails, lumber, towsacks full of grain, wooden crates of peaches, and crockery filled to the brim with molasses. But his most precious item, the surprise gift for Elizabeth he carried concealed inside a handkerchief in his shirt pocket.

The ride home was as familiar to William as the trails of his own farm, crisscrossing over hillocks and streams he'd made his way over hundreds of times. When he was within a mile of his destination, William knew he'd arrive in plenty of time for supper. Thirsty and a bit stiff, he stopped and climbed off the wagon, more tired than he should be he thought. He secured the reins of his horse to a nearby sturdy sapling and bent down to cup his hands for refreshment from the cold, clear stream. In that very instant, sharp pain seized his heart. Immediately William fell, face down, into the water.

November 9
Present Day

Etta ran her fingers over the intricate design, amazed by the closely sewn, tiny stitches. She asked, "Grandma Libby, was this made by hand, and not by machine?"

"You're correct, dear," her grandmother answered. "In those days, fine needlework was prized as an art. The more minutely stitches were sewn, the more expert the seamstress."

Etta placed the coverlet back across the foot of her grandmother's bed.

"I don't see how I'll ever get that good," she confessed.

"Oh, you can and will, as long as you practice, but all in good time. Why don't you come and sit beside me on the sofa with your scrap of material, needle, and thread, and I'll teach you a new stitch to practice this week. When you return next Saturday, you can show me your finished samples. I'm confident we'll both see your improvement by then."

Etta had spent every Saturday with her Grandma Libby for as long as she could remember. Though her friends interests seemed occupied by the latest technology game, Etta delighted over ways her grandma made stories about her ancestors come to life. Indeed, Grandma Libby was not one to passively sit and tell a story but dramatized them in extraordinary ways. Why Etta never forgot the day her grandma opened the door dressed in 1860 attire with hooped skirt and parasol as she led her to a table set for tea. On another occasion, her grandma schemed up a scavenger hunt that eventually took her to an old trunk filled with antique valentines. Etta sat spellbound as she drew individual designs, all unique while Grandma Libby told her story after story about her predecessors.

Today, however, Etta was up to the challenge of handwork and attempted to follow her grandmother's example when all at once, she pricked her finger, and a drop of blood soiled the material.

"Oh, Grandma Libby, look what I've done! Didn't I see an old thimble in that special box you have? May I use it to cover my finger while I sew?" Etta queried.

"Now I don't think I ever told you why I kept that thimble locked away," her grandma responded.

Etta brought to mind the stories her cousin Quinn recounted about her grandmother's special box. He'd boasted to Etta of its documents and old letters that brought history alive to him. And now she couldn't imagine the significance an old silver thimble held, but significant it must be to be locked up with her other family treasures.

"Don't worry about a little stain on that material scrap," her grandma continued.

"I'll let you use one of these plastic thimbles for now. And you're right, the thimble in my box is an antique with a story all its own. Fingers have filled its small form over many generations. Today, I'll tell you the thimble's story, and when you return next week, I'll take it down for you to examine more carefully."

Grandma Libby's country home wasn't much more than a cabin. Built in the 1930s, it stood on a hill with a winding gravel road that led up to it. Barely five rooms in all, the dwelling might give an outsider the appearance of tight quarters, but appearances aren't all they seem. Inside those rooms, Etta experienced not only the present but the past through stories her grandmother told her. Those experiences decorated her mind with room after room of memories Etta knew she'd recall for a lifetime.

While Grandma Libby secured a Band-Aid around her granddaughter's finger, she said, "Etta, you know I was even younger than you when I mistook the thimble for a tiny bell. Oh, I was probably eight years old, and on that day the ladies of the house were all in my grandmother's kitchen. Suddenly, I noticed a bracelet on my great grandmother Smith's arm. While we sat around the table I became distracted by the silver chain and dangling object that jingled whenever Mama Smith moved. Intrigued, I asked her, 'Mama Smith, is that a bell attached to your bracelet?' Now my great-grandmother was already very old at the time, probably in her nineties. But her memory was sharp, and she was keen to tell us stories about her childhood in Kentucky. I sat in fascination of her while she spoke. As I studied Mama Smith's features, I branded them into my memory. Her skin was like parchment paper. If you looked at her hands, her blue veins showed through distinctly. She wore her white hair in tight waves, and her cheeks were always rosy from the creamy rouge she applied. But it was her voice I loved about her best of all. It had a song-like quality to it; low in tone, accompanied by an occasional quiver. What she told me about the thimble only took minutes yet I remember it as clearly as if it was yesterday."

Etta studied Grandma Libby's face and saw her eyes brighten as she recalled that day from long ago. Her Grandma said, "Etta, let me open the window on a day in my childhood so you can view more clearly what I mean. It was Christmas 1961 when Mama Smith beckoned me to her side. She held out her frail arm so I could inspect the bracelet around her wrist. Here's her story just as she told me: 'Oh Libby my dear…come over here and let me show you. It's not a bell but a thimble. Here,' and she took the trinket off her arm. 'See, there's nothing inside to give it a ring sound, but if you look carefully above the scrollwork, there's a tiny initial, an E for Elizabeth. That stood for my great-grandmother, Elizabeth Shortridge.'

Grandma Libby paused, then continued, "Mama Smith's eyes locked with mine as she let me journey back into her past with words only she could speak in that tremulous voice of hers: 'Libby, I was probably ten years old when I first noticed the thimble on my mother's dressing table. That was the year 1885. Upon my discovery, my mother, Pamela Elizabeth, acknowledged my interest when she saw me try on the thimble. I mistakenly thought it hers with only her middle initial engraved there. Quickly, she corrected my assertion stating it was older than I realized and not hers at all. She explained how, as a young girl, she used to spend hours sewing alongside her grandmother, Elizabeth Shortridge. Staring at the thimble, I wondered about its original owner. That day was my first introduction to great-grandmother Elizabeth since she'd died many years before I was born. Not a photograph existed of her, so while mother clasped my hand, she escorted me to the bed. Comfortably seated on her feather mattress, my mother revealed how a simple sterling thimble became the priceless treasure of her grandmother, Elizabeth:'

"During the Civil War, my parents owned a hotel and tavern in Calhoun, Kentucky, along the Green River. My father's mother, Elizabeth Shortridge, came to live with us for a time since it was dangerous for widows to be alone on a farm. She helped my mother launder the bed linens and make the guests beds. But her favorite work was with needle and thread. I witnessed Grandmother Shortridge often sitting in a rocking chair, mending feather pillows, linens, and other types of handwork. One day, she asked me to fetch her sewing basket when I saw her pull from the left pocket of her dress, this thimble. We worked awhile sewing together, and when finished, I gathered our needlework to put away. Quickly, I took the thimble and placed it beside the other sewing notions within the basket,

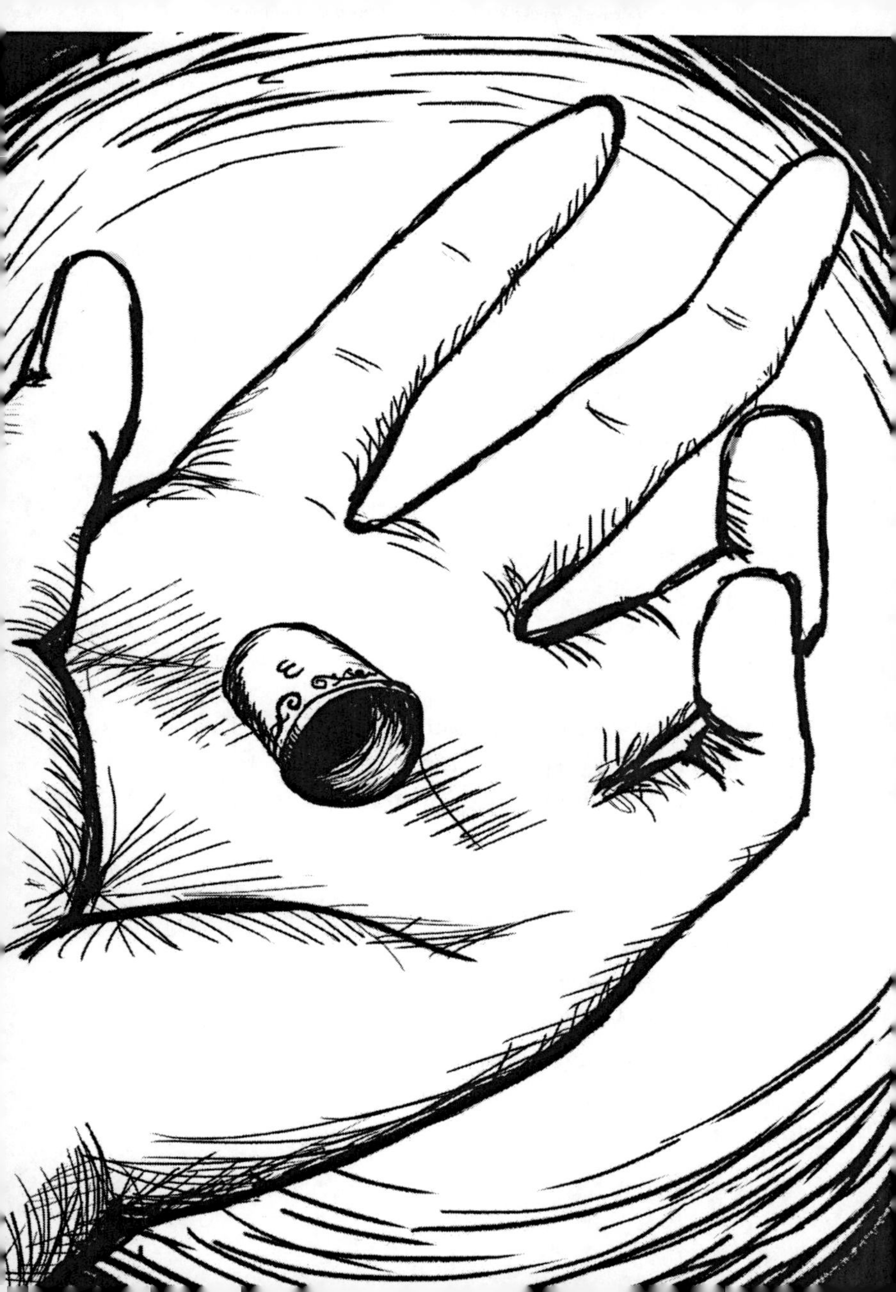

but Grandmother Elizabeth gently scolded me and said, 'Dear, the thimble goes here,' and she tapped the pocket over her heart. Naturally I asked, 'Why don't you put it away grandmother?' She said, 'My dear, this thimble is very special because it was the last gift your grandfather gave me…see, he had an *E* engraved there just for me. When he died, I found the thimble wrapped inside a handkerchief in his breast pocket. He passed away precisely one day before my forty-ninth birthday. Ever since, I've always seen my dresses have a pocket on the left side, so his gift is ever close to my heart.'"

November 16
Present day

Etta was ecstatic. It was Saturday, and at last she'd touch Grandma Libby's special thimble, slip its form over her finger and feel the connection to her ancestor, Elizabeth Shortridge.

"Etta, this thimble will be yours one day. I removed it from the bracelet years ago," Grandma Libby said as she handed it over for me to inspect.

"You're the ninth generation since Elizabeth Shortridge took it from William's pocket. Now you know why this thimble holds a significant place inside my box."

Later that evening, Etta drifted into a deep sleep and dreamt...

******

"William, do you have the list I gave you of supplies to purchase?"

"Upon my word, upon my word, Elizabeth, I'll carry your precious list over my heart!"

"Well then, get on with you. Please don't linger too long in Owensboro tomorrow. I'll have supper waiting for you."

"Why, Elizabeth, I'll be able to smell your good cooking a mile outside Owensboro! Ole Fleetfoot will see I get home to you, don't you worry!"

******

A thimble just like the one portrayed in the story was passed down to the author from her great-aunt Elizabeth. She was given it by her mother, Frances. Frances's mother, Pamela Elizabeth, was possibly the original owner; or, as believed by the author but cannot be proven, the thimble originated with Pamela's grandmother, Elizabeth Shortridge.

Wyatt's Discovery

"WYATT, DO YOU ever wonder what brings a person onto the stage of life just when needed most?" Wyatt studied his grandma's pensive mood as she looked out the window to watch snow cover the ground in a blanket of white. Cardinals, plump from generous feeders punctuated the frosty carpet with brilliant color. A log in the woodstove crackled and brought her attention back to the family tree chart set before them. His grandmother continued, "I find it intriguing that precisely when some individuals go through a trial their character is strengthened, and they're able to perform a task destined only for them."

Grandma Libby pointed and tapped on a name written on the family tree, "If Gabriel May hadn't fought in the War of 1812, he wouldn't have been awarded bounty land and left Virginia." She sighed and went on. "Who knows then? A house near a battlefield; some enemy wounded soldiers and gold coins wouldn't have been in Gabriel's future."

"Grandma Libby, tell me! What do you mean: wounded soldiers, a battlefield, and gold coins?" Wyatt asked.

"Oh, it's too long to tell, but not to read," she responded. "My grandfather used to take me to Mt. Elba, where a Civil War battle took place; the very one, near Gabriel's home.

Little by little over the years, pieces of the story came to me through my grandfather's revelations as well as what I learned from older relatives, local histories, and research. Eventually, I put it together in a story. Would you like to read it?"

"Of course!" Wyatt said eagerly.

Grandma Libby walked to a bookshelf built into the corner of the room and pulled some papers from under a small metal lockbox. Quincy, her yellow tabby, followed her every move, then perched on her lap as she sat next to Wyatt.

"Take it home, and read it on a day just like this," Grandma Libby said as she pointed to the serene, pastoral landscape outside. "Imagine yourself back in time with the characters, your ancestors. And remember to ask yourself, 'Might there be a lesson here for me?'"

And so, the following Saturday night, after Wyatt finished helping his dad with the chores around the farm, he sat down to read.

Life's stories should never be told in a hurry. This one begins with a set of twins, a baptism, and an accident.

August 19, 1826
Gravel Hill, New Jersey

Gilbert Colfax stood far enough away, supposing himself unnoticed while his brother and sister-in-law waited their turn of immersion. All at once, the bleak, murky sky opened, and a shaft of sunlight painted the scene below him with a celestial glow. Barely perceptible were the words spoken by the minister as he and the deacon held shoulders and backs of each participant slowly descending into the water, "With the confession of your sins, the old life is washed away, for he that believes in Him, a new life begins."

Gilbert loved his brother deeply but couldn't be more different in personality and character, though an identical twin. He'd not have been seen near a church service, let alone a baptizing such as this one unless he desperately needed a favor from Silas. Pursuers, hot on his trail might fall for the deception he'd prepared for them, but Gilbert couldn't risk any overconfidence. Looking on, he yearned impatiently for the ceremony down the hill to end.

At last, the minister's words rang out to signal the close of the service: "And now in the words of Paul the Apostle, 'In whom ye are buried with Him in baptism, wherein also ye are risen with Him through the faith of the operation of God, who hath raised Him from the dead.' (1) Go. Live out godly lives reflecting His glory. Blessed be the name of the Lord! Amen."

Perspiration not only ran down Gilbert's face and torso but on the palms of his hands as he raced to catch up with Silas and Isadora, just as they stepped into a carriage pointed toward home.

"Gilbert! You're a sight for sore eyes. However did you find us here?" Silas asked as he patted his coat still soggy from the creek water. "You don't have a confession to make do you, dear brother? I'm sure our pastor would come back for one more sinner."

"Not hardly, Silas. I just need a place to relax before my long journey west. You wouldn't care if I stayed a night with you before I travel onward?" Gilbert asked.

"Just where west are you headed, brother? Say, you've put on some weight since I last saw you."

At this, Isadora interrupted, "Now, Silas, that's no way to treat your brother whom you've not seen in an age! Of course, Gilbert, you may stay as long as you wish," she said. Though an uncomfortable silence fell between the brothers for an instant, Isadora broke the spell with her cheerful conversation for the remainder of the ride.

Later that evening, Gilbert slipped off his coat, heavy with gold coins he'd sewn in hidden pockets and fell into bed, too exhausted to wash up. *I'll just bathe in the creek behind the house come morning,* he thought as he slipped into a sound, yet fitful sleep.

Before anyone stirred, Gilbert tiptoed quietly at dawn to clean away dirt from his body and map out a plan to journey ahead of the men on his trail. Just as he pulled up his trousers, he heard a scream coming from Silas' home. He sprinted quickly as possible, only to find Isadora weeping uncontrollably.

"Some men charged in and took Silas with them." She gasped. "They kept saying, 'Colfax, where's our money?' When he said he didn't know what they were talking about, they struck him. Naturally to protect you, Silas said, 'Alright, I'll show you,' so they took him. Whatever have you done, Gilbert?"

Gilbert was barely thirty-three, but an elderly gloom cast a shadow over his heart, like frost that conceals ground beneath it. He'd been plotting a life of ease, yet a fissure in his flawed judgment began to emerge. Quickly, he denounced it. Even in this dilemma, Gilbert gripped tightly to what he understood buried deep within him as wrong, only to remain unheeded.

"I'll find him, Isadora, and bring him home to you, I promise. Whatever you do, take my suit coat and hide it. There's enough money in hidden pockets for you and Silas to live on comfortably," he paused, "for a long time."

"Oh no! No!" Isadora cried, but he'd already dashed out the door.

Six hours later, Gilbert concentrated on calming down to recover his breath from the strenuous ride he gave his brother's horse. Racing hard to find him, he thought he heard something close to the path ahead. Quietly as he could he dismounted, tied the reins and crept forward in the direction of the sound. As he came closer to a clearing in the woods, voices were heard.

"Poor fellow. Looks as if his neck was broken when he fell from the horse," one man said.

"No, this man didn't fall. I saw him pushed by those other men when they realized we were too close. We'll have to find out if he has any family around here. Let's grab the blanket from my horse and wrap him; then, we'll head back in the direction of their approach. I've no doubt Hull and Freer will catch up with the men who did this," the man in charge spoke.

An overwhelming flood of emotion hit Gilbert as he realized the men spoke words over his dead brother's body meant for him. In a brief instant, his guilt almost made him come forward, but suddenly the pull to draw back from the scene was too strong. And so, Gilbert stole away, once again. Not to the east, nor to the west, but south.

Bradley County, Arkansas

Somewhere from the haze of infancy, a love of horses developed. John Porter Hobson couldn't remember the exact moment the connection he made with horse and himself materialized, but he thought it might have been on the journey his family took from Mississippi to Arkansas.

September 14, 1849

Sitting on a wagon bench while his father drove horses through rutty roads, John appreciated the animals, even from their backsides, as they obeyed his father's commands. The horse's power, if unleashed, concealed a strength that could bring a man down. Despite that, God purposed this creature to be, in essence, gentle.

And so John found fitting the only words he remembered his father telling him before he died were those spoken on that wagon bench, about horses.

"Remember, my boy, 'horses fly without wings and conquer without swords.'" (2)

Three months later, as shoveled dirt hit his father's coffin, John stood between his mother, Mary, and grandfather, Gabriel May, until the hollow sound of dirt on wood vanished. Later, John followed the couple back to his grandfather's home. With orchards to its east, two stories stood between brick chimneys. Wide porches extended from front, to back; though the rear porch had been enclosed to make an extra room the previous year. Giant post oaks shaded the yard in front with a garden, barn, and smokehouse behind them.

Gabriel May was born in Pittsylvania County, Virginia, in 1792 and spent his early adulthood there. As the son of a revolutionary patriot, he didn't question the call to arms for a second time with England in 1812. Soon after the war, he married and raised eleven children and was later given a land warrant of 160 acres in southern Arkansas.

His friends and neighbors said of him, "Gabriel May is a man of principle." Whether this was due to his belief in God, having read the Bible through several times as witnessed by his family, or from his conviction that faith should be seen, not only heard, was the legacy that carried stories told by his descendants long after he passed. Regardless the reason, Gabriel was known as a man whose word was his bond.

Years passed, and the absence of John's father lingered heavily in the world around him as he followed his Papa May like a shadow about the farm. Under his grandfather's tutelage, John learned the rudiments to maintain a clean barn for tools and animals alike. He especially took pride in keeping stalls meticulous, knowing this met Papa May's approval. In moments of performing these mundane chores, visions of John's father returned to him: first by his voice, then brief glimpses of a face in delight, or sometimes anger, and even death.

Though John still had his mother, her domestic duties kept her so busy from sunup to sundown she couldn't provide the nurturing most mothers demonstrated. What John's mother couldn't furnish as nurturer, his grandfather made up for in companionship. There were afternoons of fishing along the Saline, wagon rides to the mill to trade butchered meat for flour, or runs to the smithies to have a new implement forged for the farm.

One particular day as he neared home with his grandfather, John confessed, "Papa May, I'm afraid a day might come when I won't remember how my father looked. Even now, my memories of him are starting to fade."

His grandfather didn't answer right away, and John thought his silence meant agreement, but instead Papa May weighed his words carefully before he spoke.

"John, time may erase some of your memories, but in you are traces of your father. You share some of those traits, by your appearance as well as character. The Bible tells us, 'Remember the days of old, and consider the years of many generations; ask thy father, and he will shew thee; thy elders, and they will tell thee.'(3) Your father may not be here to show you, but I can for him, and I'll tell you about his days on this earth though they were few," said Papa May.

In time, John became acquainted with the person of his father through his grandfather's stories about him. Understanding the serious yet dutiful nature of his grandson, Papa May intuitively recognized John's keen mind and love for horses. Given that, his grandfather groomed in him an ability to understand and appreciate this magnificent animal.

One hot July afternoon, five years later, a stranger rode to the farm on a beautiful dapple gray stallion just as eleven-year-old John walked out the barn. The rider looked tired and disheveled, but his horse was sleek and magnificent. The stranger was the first to speak, "Is your father at home, young man?"

John didn't have time to respond. Papa May stepped onto the front porch and asked, "What can I do for you, mister?"

"Bean's my name, Mr. Bean. I've ridden many miles and would appreciate a place to rest, as well as feed and water my horse if that's all right with you?" the man answered.

"And I'm Gabriel May. Yes, we've a room on the back side of the house. You're welcome to stay."

Mr. Bean dismounted and offered the reins of his horse to John. "Would you see Gray Eagle is brushed and combed, son? He could use a good grooming."

"Gray Eagle's a fine animal, sir. I'd be honored to take care of him for you. We have plenty of room in the barn," John said as his hand stroked the horse's neck. "And I'll see that he's fed."

"That'd be fine," Mr. Bean said with a decidedly northern accent.

To John, Gray Eagle was the handsomest specimen of a horse he'd ever seen. Just as Mr. Bean released the animal, he bent down with his eyes fixed on the boy and addressed him with a hush that seemed to convey a shared secret. "If you can spare some feed, I'd appreciate it, but I noticed that prime pasture on my way in; he can graze there once you've seen to grooming him. Ole Eagle boy here likes to be talked to while he's brushed," he said, then reached up to pull off the saddle and handed it to him. "He'll be your friend forever if you comb out his mane and tail." With a swagger, Mr. Bean ambled toward the house while he carried a saddlebag over his shoulder.

John wasn't sure what to think of Mr. Bean, but he didn't dwell on it. In fact, it drifted out his mind as quickly as the screech of an owl. Neither was he one to analyze peculiarities of strangers since it wasn't uncommon for Papa May to take one in on occasion as they passed through the area. He only knew this impressive horse was under his charge, and he'd see to it that he befriended him.

Mr. Bean, who looked much the same age as Papa May, sat at the table that evening dressed in a white shirt, dark trousers held up by suspenders, and a vest of woven plaid. After the meal, John joined his grandfather and guest on the front porch while they reminisced over stories of their youth. Listening in, John learned how Mr. Bean lived a life constantly on the move, always enamored by the adventure of what might be just beyond the horizon. With a tinge of disappointment, John resigned himself to believe he wouldn't be able to groom and care for Gray Eagle long since Mr. Bean would likely be on his way come morning. But the predictableness of human nature sometimes takes an unexpected turn, and then the plans of a habitual wanderer may change altogether.

Hours later, John roused to shuffling feet and moans, mixed with the soft voices of his mother and Papa May sometime in the wee hours of the day. Thinking he was in a dream, he fell back to sleep.

Meanwhile, Papa May and Mary were occupied with a delirious Mr. Bean, whose cries awakened them not long after they slept. The fever didn't break come morning, or the morning after, as they took turns keeping vigil by his side. On occasion, their guest spewed incoherent speech, but other times revealed lucid, rational statements, all the while, unaware his hosts understood most every word.

Naturally, John took advantage of this unexpected interval with Gray Eagle. Following his daily chores, he rode the steed through terrain as yet unexplored by him on Papa May's farm. At times in the wide-open fields, he was convinced Gray Eagle drank the wind when his nostrils flared with the excitement of a hearty run. John relished these quiet moments he shared while saddled above Gray Eagle as he listened to sounds in the forest.

On the fifth day, Mr. Bean's condition improved. Suddenly, he awoke to a snoring man beside his bed.

"Where, where am I?" he queried.

Startled, Papa May jerked awake, "Say, my friend! Why, you look alert but had us mighty worried these past few days. Let me call Mary to bring you a bowl of broth. I believe you've decided not to leave this world yet, or at least the Lord doesn't want you to," Papa May said in all seriousness.

Mr. Bean tried to sit up in bed, but collapsed and allowed his hosts to tend to him. Too weak to walk or take care of his most essential needs, he was compelled to receive this family's help. Dependence wasn't a trait he valued, but the circumstances now forced on him produced a reliance he seldom experienced. During his recovery, John often sat next to his bed and described in detail experiences he shared with Gray Eagle. Since the backroom once was a porch, it now afforded many windows, and at times, John rode Gray Eagle to an opened one beside Mr. Bean so he could reach out his arm and pet the animal. In his observations, John realized how much older Mr. Bean looked after his illness. As days turned to weeks, Mr. Bean developed a limp in his gait that hadn't been there before.

Long hours spent between Papa May and his guest in private conversations suddenly stopped whenever John came into their presence. Moreover, John found, to his amazement, an alteration in Mr. Bean's personality. It wasn't something he noticed overnight, but when he reflected on it, he understood a relationship had formed between his grandfather and Mr. Bean that became more like a brother to brother.

As time went on, a custom began that only Mr. Bean walked down the lane to pick up mail for the household. On appointed days, the mail carrier rode his horse and deposited it in a leather bag on a fence post at the entrance of the May property. Mr. Bean's habit may have started by way of recovery but remained on as his duty. So much so that he always insisted, rain or shine with a cane in hand, that he, and he only, retrieved the mail. One late afternoon, John sat on Gray Eagle and noticed Mr. Bean, whose back faced him, rifle through letters only to place one of them inside his shirt pocket. At the horse's snort, the old man turned, waved at John and started his slow walk back toward the house.

As the months passed, Mr. Bean was no longer considered a guest in their home but rather a part of the family. That transformation was as natural as the relationship between John and Gray Eagle. Initially groomed to ride the horse until Mr. Bean traveled on his way, John had bonded with the animal to the point that Gray Eagle seemed to prefer approaching him first whenever they were together outdoors. One autumn evening, while the family sat on the front porch listening to the call of the whip-poor-will, Mr. Bean surprised John.

"There's something I want to tell you, young man," he said.

"Yes, sir?"

"You've taken such care of Gray Eagle these many months, I want you to have him. I've seen all the world I care to see. I believe I've found a home, and I know Gray Eagle has too," he said with tears in his eyes.

"You don't mean that Mr. Bean! Thank you! I can save up some money to pay for him," John said with sincere gratitude.

"No, boy, I'm giving him to you," he said firmly.

The reality that Mr. Bean was part of the family didn't just begin and end in the May household but was illuminated to those in the community as well. This revelation came home to John one day as he stood beside his grandfather on an errand in town. A merchant asked, "Say, Gabriel May, how can you let that stranger stay in your home when you know nothing about where he's from or what he may be hiding?"

As always was his tact, Papa May took a moment before he responded, "Mr. Bean's welcome in my home as long as he wants to stay, and I've no cause to hold over him what may be in his past. If I can be salt that causes a thirst in him and point his way to the master of the universe, then I'll gladly share what crumbs fall from my table with a stranger."

So Mr. Bean lived with the May's until his death six years later. While John and his mother searched through what few personal effects were in Mr. Bean's possession, John found a small envelope, well-worn with a letter inside, written in delicate handwriting:

> My dear Gilbert,
>
> As you can see, I respected your wishes and addressed this letter to a "Mr. Bean."With regard to your entreaty, I want you to know, however, I forgave you long ago. The night my dear Silas was brought home to me, I buried him in your suit coat laden with gold. There was no need to hold

bitterness or rancor toward you. I've spent years praying God would use the circumstances that led to Silas's death to bring you to Him. Perhaps after all the years of running, Gilbert, you'll realize the depth of God's love for you. How could I, a sinner in God's eyes, not grant forgiveness to you? Thank you for writing after all this time. It is my deepest prayer you discover the peace that only He can give.

With all my heart,
Isadora

John placed the letter back inside its envelope and tucked it into the shirt pocket of a Mr. Bean, in peace. He was buried in the May family plot, along with the prayers of those who came to love him.

April 29, 1863

With the countryside in the grips of the Civil War over two years, John felt the pang to join his State's defense almost from the beginning. But his aging grandfather and vulnerable mother would be left to fend for themselves in such hostility. So John stayed on the farm and did most of the work of two men.

One day John was away placing traps along the Saline River when a group of bushwhackers rode up to the May farm and confiscated mules, wagons, and equipment to carry off for their use. As they were about to leave, one of them saw Gray Eagle grazing in the lower meadow. Papa May realized what was about to happen and called after the man to stop. "That horse is too old! Please! Don't take him. He's my grandson's favorite," he said.

"Why, he looks good enough to pull a wagon. Besides, old man, this is war. My men need every four-footed beast we can find, and that means your grandson's horse is now ours," he said.

Four hours later, a weary John approached the back path leading to the farm. As he neared the fence, he whistled for Gray Eagle and wondered why the horse didn't respond. Quickening his pace, he scanned the area around the barn thinking his grandfather must have placed the horse in the corral. A surreal silence cloaked the landscape surrounding the site. Silence, so heavy, John sensed his desperation rise.

Once inside the house, the faces of Papa May and his mother told him his suspicions were true. Even without words, he knew something dreadful happened. "Son, war is in our backyard now and requires a toll be taxed upon us. We may have lost a part of what brings us our livelihood, but we still have our farm and our lives. I'm just sorry they took Gray Eagle. I tried to talk them out of it, but it was no use."

"Who were they, and where did they go? How long have they been gone?" John cried.

"It was before noon, son," Papa May answered. "And they're scoundrels posing as military. Besides, they're miles from here by now. Who knows? They've probably made it to Louisiana by now."

"If I'd been here this wouldn't have happened," John said in anger.

"If you'd been here," his mother said, "They'd have taken you!"

"Not if I could help it. At least I'd have hidden Gray Eagle," John said indignantly.

In a matter of months, John acquired enough used equipment and animals to replace some of what the May farm had lost. He also arranged for one of his uncles to come and watch over the farm after he left. And so without a word to his mother or Papa May, John slipped off one day before dawn to volunteer in the Confederate Cavalry.

March 30, 1864

Despite the day beginning like any other for Gabriel May, it ended far different. His son Thomas, whose farm neighbored his own, divided his time between them as much as possible. Still, after almost a year, Gabriel's farm started to show signs of disrepair following John's absence. He missed the boy though he knew John was very much a man now, and he wondered about him continually. The sting of *no good-bye* hurt, but Gabriel knew John must come to terms with the circumstances life dealt him.

As he closed the door on the hen house, Gabriel's bleary eyes glanced westward toward the road, and saw the Southern Army headed straight for Mt. Elba. In the hours that followed, it was evident the Yankees were there, very much, to greet them. The battle didn't last long, but was bloody nonetheless, and the Confederate army fled all over Gabriel's woods, stampeded by their enemy.

Gabriel's home, so close to the battle, was conveniently requisitioned as a hospital. The wounded from both armies were brought there. Mary and Papa May labored alongside the surgeon, as cries from the soldiers punctured the quiet long into the night. After their healthy comrades left to fight in other battles, the injured and dying alike became the task at hand for the May household. For those whose lives ended, a decent burial in the May family plot was afforded them.

By now, though nearly seventy-two years of age, Gabriel recognized a purpose that invigorated him. What some viewed as hard luck that his home was so close to a battle, Gabriel deemed as divine destiny. He prayed for the speedy recovery of the lame and gave Christian burials for the dying, no matter what color their uniform. This deed was brought to the attention of a Yankee officer who made a visit to the May farm weeks later. As he rode with a company of soldiers pulling ambulance wagons, Major William Dowd of the Federal army addressed Gabriel, who had stepped onto the porch.

"Sir, I'd like to speak with a Gabriel May, if you please?" he asked, expecting a younger man.

"That'd be me," Gabriel stated matter-of-factly.

Surprised, the officer went on, "We're here to collect our wounded, but I understand there were four of our soldiers who died in your care. Would you show me where you've buried them?"

Gabriel led the officer away from the group while Mary allowed the rest of his command to load the injured into their wagons. Not entirely sure the act of a decent burial was true, Major Dowd followed Gabriel behind the house toward a grove of walnut trees which shaded the headstones.

"You know, Major, I was in the army many years ago. A different kind of war, but war just the same. And when you listen to a man's dying words, they're not about the fierceness of the battle he's just fought in, or how unjust he may feel that his body stopped the bullet." Gabriel paused to bring emphasis on what he was about to say. "His dying words are of a family he's left behind and the God he's about to meet. Major, I listened to the parting words of your men, and it was my honor to bury them alongside my family."

"I don't know how to thank you Mr. May, and I know the families of these men would feel the same gratitude as I. Before I leave, if you'll accompany me to my horse I have something I want to give you," Major Dowd said.

The officer knew only one way to express his appreciation for the compassion displayed his men but realized from their brief time together Gabriel would likely refuse it. Once beside his chestnut stallion, the Major said, "Sir, here is something for you, only promise not to open it until I'm out of sight. Do I have your word?"

"Yes, young man, I suppose I can do that," Gabriel answered reluctantly, as he took a small leather pouch from the soldier. "Godspeed Major, may the war end soon to rejoin you with your family. Where do you call home?"

"Wisconsin, Mr. May, and thank you again," he answered tapping the edge of his officer's blue hat.

An hour later, Gabriel opened the leather bag onto the May kitchen table and knew why the Major wanted him to wait. He'd never have accepted such a gift, and now he'd have to contemplate long and hard what to do with it.

April 26, 1864
Camden, Arkansas

"Gentlemen, I've called this council of war to ponder our situation deeply," Union General Steele stated as he looked at the grim faces of the officers: Thayer, Salomon, and Carr.

"A handful of our men made away from that debacle of Marks's Mill yesterday and have informed me Fagan has roughly three thousand troops last seen headed north. Do you realize the precarious situation we find ourselves? I estimate ten to fifteen thousand enemy troops have their jaws ready to bite. We can forget the march to Shreveport! That's out of the question now. As I see it, we've only three options: surrender, starvation, or exodus back to Little Rock. What will it be gentlemen?"

Brigadier General Eugene Carr, Steele's Cavalry commander, advised flight but urged it must be done within twenty-four hours in order to be successful. Also, he recommended sutlers wagons be destroyed as their rations were scant and would only slow retreat. "Issue the troops two crackers of hardtack and a little cornmeal with the admonition that's all they'll get till they make it to Little Rock. I don't know what will make a soldier move faster on the march than his growling belly," Carr snickered.

General Steele continued, "We must have our units work from dawn until dusk, this day, to load wagons and destroy any nonessential equipment with as little smoke and sound as possible. I don't want our strategy to alert the enemy in his camp nearby. And, I want all the infantry to break their step that will muffle any march as they exit."

Brigadier General Frederick Salomon broke in, "Sir, we could make use of that baled cotton along the docks. I'll assign a company to wrap the wheels of wagons with it to maximize stratagem."

"Excellent, Salomon," General Steele said. "And order our rearguard to leave lanterns alight. Furthermore, I want drums to roll taps to an empty camp by eight o'clock, understood?"

"Yes, General," they all said in unison.

"Now are you ready to study the map? We need to decide the best course to take," Steele finished.

A little while later, General Steele had one last trick up his sleeve. He called a sergeant into his tent and asked all those present to leave.

"Are you willing to perform a dangerous duty for your country, soldier?" the general asked.

"Yes, sir," said the sergeant without hesitation.

"I want you to dress in an enemy uniform and go behind their lines. Entering General Fagan's camp, you are to carry a message only for him. Explain how you've learned the plans of the enemy and hand him these *intercepted* papers signed by me stating our march to Shreveport. Yours will be a hazardous mission and might fail. Are you still willing to do it?"

"It would be my honor to follow your orders, sir."

"You're a brave soldier sergeant, and I'll award you if you succeed," the general said as he put a firm hand on his shoulder.

After he left, the general only shook his head and smiled where the sergeant had been.

Dawn surfaced on the horizon of April 28th, as the Confederate army began its pursuit of their enemy. In hopes of overtaking the camp the previous day, the southerners found it empty, except for deserted equipment staging that impression. Compounding their circumstances, the Southern Army couldn't cross the Ouachita River, since Yankee engineers removed the pontoons to use on another river further along the way. By the time the Confederates constructed a floating bridge to cross, their enemy was far ahead of them.

General Steele and his war council chose a different route to Little Rock over the usual one. Instead, he marched his troops on a circuitous route toward a river called Saline. Even on shortened rations, the Union Army managed to gain a day's head start on the Confederates.

On the 29th, the first of many wagons reached the river at Jenkins Ferry, where engineers launched pontoons to cross. Other details worked to construct roads in such a fashion that wheels wouldn't sink in the boggy clay. Rains came down in sheets so hard, mules foundered with engulfed wagons too heavy to move forward. But their headstart gave them time to build stout embankments to crouch behind once the enemy appeared.

The following day, the rain stopped, but a new menace hampered the soldiers: sheets of milky, white fog. It was around eight o'clock in the morning when Private John Porter Hobson found himself in some of the fiercest fightings he'd yet to encounter. Ordered to dismount and halt, he overheard a commanding officer say to another, "By God, where is Fagan? Summoning the navy? He could have thrown himself on the enemy's front if he'd caught up with Steele before he reached the Saline! It shouldn't have taken him this long to join in the fight."

The rest of his tirade was drowned out by the directive of his officer, "Charge, men! We've got fog on our side."

Lying low behind a parapet, a soldier in blue had his gun aimed at the ready. Haze halted no shots, nor demanded a sniper's marksmanship. And that instant, a sharpshooter's minie ball pierced the right leg of Private John P. Hobson.

July 15, 1864

John prodded his horse to a canter and spoke as easily to the animal as to a friend, "Rambler; we're almost home. It's been a year since I've seen the place, and I wonder if Uncle Tom kept it up for Mother and Papa May." The healing of his wound was slow, but the excitement to be there overshadowed any effect he felt from it.

At the May farm, his mother sat on a porch rocker while she shelled lima beans and hummed a melody sparked from a childhood memory. Meadowlarks rivaled her song in the overgrown hay field next to the house. So lost in her task, she didn't see the rider approach in the distance. It wasn't until John yelled that Mary jarred from her musings. Recognizing his voice, she leapt without heeding the bowl in her lap and shelled beans scattered in every direction. Her hand went to her mouth, and she gasped at the shock of seeing her son. Mary wanted to run to him but didn't trust her rheumy legs or the sudden giddy lightheadedness that rushed through her soul.

John urged Rambler to race the distance when he saw his mother stand. Shortly in front of her, he shifted his weight carefully to dismount but winced from the smart of his slow-to-heal wound. Once his legs found their purchase, he turned and hobbled up to embrace her.

"Where's Papa May?" he asked, surprised by his absence. A little hesitant, she answered, "Papa died last week, son. Dr. Chandler said it was dropsy. There was nothing more he could do for him. He died in his sleep. His old body started to fail shortly after the battle here, at Mt. Elba," she said as she pointed to the woods beyond. "I wish you could've seen how he helped those wounded and dying men," she finished.

Mary witnessed the impact her words had on her son. Perceptive John needed to bear his grief privately, she went on, "Why don't you go and visit his grave? He's buried next to Grandma. There's something he left for you in his room when you're ready. I'll prepare some dinner, but go, take as long as you need."

The walk around the house to Papa May's grave felt as arduous as any cavalry charge he attempted the past year. John no longer fought back the emotions and let his tears fall as he looked down at the fresh grave of the man who was more like a father to him. Flooded with guilt for his unspoken goodbye a year ago, John wobbly knelt at the foot of the grave and grasped a handful of recently mounded red clay. "I love you, Papa May," were the only words he could utter.

An hour later, his mother asked him over dinner how he acquired his injury. John only had to say "Jenkins Ferry," and she knew the horror of what he went through from the accounts widely spread about the battle.

"I want to go in his room," John said as he pushed the plate away from him, still half full of generous portions.

"Go right on ahead, son. But let me show you the letter he left for you," Mary said as she walked to her father's roll-top desk and unlatched it. Within was an array of compartments neatly filled with papers, ink bottles, and letters, all opened, except one; addressed to John P.

After his mother had closed the door to clear away the dinner table, John sat in the desk chair to read what his grandfather thought important to tell him. He knew enough about Papa May's character that no words of judgment or condemnation would drift from his message, even though he felt that was his due. John pushed a stray lock of hair behind his ear and began to read:

> June 17, 1864
> My beloved John,
>
> I was already advanced in years when your need of a fatherly influence became paramount to your rearing. I promised your father as he lay dying I'd raise you as one of my own, and I believe I kept that promise.
>
> My time is close and I write these words knowing that I'll not have the privilege of speaking them to you since your duty to our country called you away and my old frame cannot linger long for your eventual return. Though we didn't part as I'd

have wished, I hold no grudge over your exit. I too, was once young and understand the call of a man to find his own way in life.

John, there's a cord that ties the head to the heart. If you deny it exists, you weaken the link and run the risk of not bridging the gap between them. Over my lifetime, I've sought to reach others when their trials seemed insurmountable. You'll remember our dear friend, Mr. Bean. An alias for a name that's immaterial, but one who served to represent what any one of us could be when given to the influence of an unscrupulous nature. He might well have been in and out of our lives, had it not been for the divine intervention of a debilitating infirmity. In the beginning, I understood Mr. Bean had a haunted past he could no longer run from, and his arrival on our doorstep was an opportunity to minister to a broken man. In the end, I realized I was no different in the eyes of my Maker if I thought of myself more highly than I ought. He died at peace as my friend and brother in the grand race of life, which now for me will end soon as well. It's with my sincere love that I leave to you two things. The first is the key that will strengthen the tie from your head to your heart. It will carry you through any trial, any tribulation—my Bible. You should fill your mind with its pages, but the secret is to place its living words in your heart. Study it well and the Savior of the Universe will join us together again one day in the future. The second request is practical, but one I know you'll fulfill. Behind the mantel clock is a small, leather bag with twelve gold coins. One coin for each of my children, and the last one for you. Distribute them upon your return. The story of how they came to me, your mother will tell you. All that is left is my property, which may be sold or divided among you equally, however, deemed necessary.

I loved you always,
Papa May

Wyatt put down the pages with deep appreciation for the characters whose lives he came to know reading Grandma Libby's story. She'd also handed him a package with instructions to wait until he finished the story before he unwrapped it. As he lifted the lid off the box, he saw a well-worn Bible and a silky bag with threaded drawstring. Carefully, Wyatt opened the Bible with the name, John Porter Hobson, written inside it. Then he loosened the string on the bag and dropped one gold coin into his hand. As he turned it over in his palm, he wondered, *This must have been John's—my ancestor's gold coin!*

******

Gabriel May, Mary May Hobson, and John Porter Hobson, were ancestors of the author. John Porter's father, James Fisher Hobson, died shortly after his migration from Mississippi to Arkansas around 1849–50. Gabriel May became the guardian of John Porter Hobson along with other siblings not mentioned in the story.

John Porter Hobson served in the Confederate Cavalry during the Civil War, and his grandfather's home was used as a hospital following the engagement at Mt. Elba. According to one descendant's account, a Union officer returned for the wounded following the battle and paid Gabriel May in gold coins in appreciation of the care given his soldiers. Following the war, some of the parents of those buried on his property visited their son's graves.

The mysterious Mr. Bean did exist, though he lived as a guest with a different ancestor of the author.

Scarlett's Discovery

March 9, 1893

"MARTHA, I KNOW there are ways the deaf can be taught to communicate and live productive lives. Mattie and Lura are intelligent and want to learn. I see it in their eyes when they watch Ella read her books. Ahhh, those three are inseparable. Ella will just have to understand her sisters need to board at the school in Little Rock, at least for a time, so they can learn sign language," James murmured softly, as he lay on the feather bed beside his wife.

"Oh, James, it must be done. I've tried to be a good mother and teach them how to do housework as well as care for our babies, but it's frustrating. Ella will have to get over it. Their mother would have done the same," said Martha, a bit too harshly.

James pondered his wife's bitter words in his brokenness but kept silent. It had been difficult with three young girls to raise after Sarah passed away eight years ago.

Ah, Sarah, he thought, *my sweet, beautiful Sarah.* He promised her on her deathbed he'd always provide his best for the girls. The memory of her passing, even tonight, brought tears to his eyes, and he was glad the darkness shielded him. From the beginning, James understood Sarah's concern about Mattie and Lura's handicap. At the time, it was such a mystery how Mattie was born deaf. Then came Ella, who was born without impairment, and last, Lura, who came into the world with partial deafness. But they accepted these challenges as part and parcel of life. Mattie was growing up so fast and, to boot, looked more like her mother than either of her sisters. She even inherited Sarah's sweet disposition. Just now, the thought of hurting Mattie pained James incredibly. Tomorrow he needed to mask his true feelings from Ella when he told her of the plans for her sisters.

Sarah's parting words suddenly echoed back to him: "James, I know you'll always do what's best for our girls…I want you to remarry so they'll have a mother. The burden of their raising will be too heavy for you alone."

Life, after Sarah died, hadn't been easy, so James moved from Mississippi to Arkansas to establish a new livelihood to put the past behind him. Even from the onset, there was interest in the widower and his family until the girls' handicap became more evident, and awkward glances from the opposite sex signaled unease. James was resolved to raise his family alone until the day he walked into Joseph's Dry Goods and saw Martha behind the counter. Eleven years younger and never married, she at first seemed undaunted after a short courtship and quick proposal to take on the challenge of a ready-made family. Her punctilious character and prudent management of finances seemed the perfect fit for James' new household. Following the birth of their first child, however, a change began to emerge in Martha's behavior toward Mattie and Lura. As time went by, her frustration with their disability turned into resentment. It was her insistence that drove James to take the trip to the capitol to seek information about the Arkansas Deaf-Mute Institute.

Where would he find the courage to part with his girls? Help me, Lord! He cried as he fell into sleep, exhausted.

6:00 a.m.
The following day

"Ella, I need you to be brave and set a good example for the little ones," Papa explained. "Mattie and Lura will be able to come home for visits in the summertime, so it won't be goodbye forever. Besides, if you think about it, when they come back for visits it will be like Christmas."

Ella understood Papa was trying to make her feel better, but she'd never been apart from either of them, even for a night.

"Oh, Papa, I don't know how I'll survive without them beside me. From the moment Mama passed away, our souls knit tightly together." She sighed.

"Ella, you'll have me, mother Martha, and the children here at home. Mattie and Lura will have each other. Think how happy they'll be when they learn a new way to communicate. In time, you'll be able to write letters to them once they've learned to write. Then before you know it, they can teach you sign language," Papa said consolingly.

"But, Papa, we know each other so well," Ella countered back unconvinced, "even to the depth of our thoughts."

"Dear, think of all you've learned in school. Would you deny Mattie and Lura the opportunity to learn from teachers who know a special way to teach the deaf how to read and write?" Hoping to assuage her grief he added, "It will be difficult because they're much older than most girls who start to school. Regardless, the superintendent explained to me Mattie and Lura will be so busy making new friends with other classmates who already know how to sign, they won't have time to miss home."

"I suppose, Papa," Ella answered back.

Present day

"Grandma Libby, can you tell me, who are the ladies in the old picture beside your bed?" Scarlett asked.

"Why, that's my great-grandmother Ella and her two sisters, Mattie, and Lura. Aren't they beautiful? Oh my goodness! Within that picture is a buried treasure—a story, just waiting to be discovered," Grandma Libby explained.

"What do you mean, grandma? How can you tell there's a story buried within a picture?"

"Well, dear, you have to begin with curiosity. And what do you do when you're curious about something?"

Scarlett thought a moment then responded, "I suppose you search to get clues."

"Yes you're on the right track, but before you get your clues, you need to ask the right questions and know as well, who, and where to address those questions," her Grandma Libby explained, pausing before she continued, "but the most difficult part of your search is to be patient. You don't always get answers to your questions. However, you may discover a nugget of information that opens up a storehouse of knowledge, and then you feel as if you knew them without ever having lived in their time."

"Oh, Grandma Libby, will you show me how to do it… how to find a hidden treasure in pictures?"

"Why yes, Scarlett. Bring the picture of the three sisters with you, and we'll go into my office where I have a file about the family. Then I'll show you how I uncovered their story."

As she opened the bottom drawer of her file cabinet, Grandma Libby ran her finger over the folders until she found a thick one with the name, Daisy Margaret (Mattie) Henderson. She opened it on the desk in front of Scarlett and spread out several pages of documents, letters, and last a small, thin box that looked to be a jewel case of some sort.

"What's that?" Scarlett asked pointing to the box. "Ah! We'll save it for last. But now, let's start with this." Grandma Libby pulled a copy of an application from the Arkansas Deaf-Mute Institute, dated 1893. "This was filled out by James Henderson, Mattie and Lura's father. Let's see, here it is. Cause of deafness: Unknown…Names of children to be enrolled: Mattie and Lura…Ages: Mattie–14, Lura–10. Imagine it, Scarlett. These girls were older than you, but just starting their education in a boarding school for the deaf."

Scarlett looked over the record in her grandmother's hand and could tell the copy's age not only by the written dates but the language of phrases now considered derogatory. Natural capacity: Bright, dull, stupid. Answer: Bright. White or colored: Answer: White.

"How did you get this, Grandma Libby?" Scarlett asked.

"Well, I interviewed a great-aunt many years ago, and she told me Mattie and Lura attended the Arkansas School for the Deaf, the current name for the institution. So I wrote the school and asked if they kept any archives of earlier students. Not only did they send this copy of the application, but a lovely book about the school's history," Grandma Libby answered. "Look, here in the book there's a picture of the girl's dormitory where Mattie stayed before the fire. Oh, but I'm getting ahead of myself."

"Fire! I want to hear what happened! Please tell me." Scarlett begged.

"Before we get to that," her grandma replied, "think: how difficult it must have been for their father, James, to separate his family. There's a hint, here, when he answered the questions back on the application." Scarlett focused her eyes down the page. She followed Grandma Libby's finger that pointed to the final questions: Are you able to clothe your children? Answer: No. Are you able to pay for their traveling expenses on holidays? Answer: No.

"Does that mean they had to stay at the school for Christmas?" Scarlett asked.

"I'm afraid so," her grandma answered sadly.

Scarlett closed her eyes as she concentrated on the words that painted a picture from days long ago. She imagined a scene playing out on a stage before her. Instantly, the tableau appeared more authentic than a mere play. There in front of her, boarding a train from the distant past were two girls while a father and their tearful sister, Ella, held back.

Conway Depot
March 11, 1893

The train's whistle blared one last time as Papa pulled Ella away from her sisters' embrace. Signaling the porter to seat Mattie and Lura near the door, he explained that a teacher from their school would meet them at the depot once they arrived in Little Rock.

When James recalled the last few days, it pained him to part with Sarah's wedding ring. He'd hoped to give it to Mattie one day, but the sale of it enabled the purchase of two tickets to Little Rock with the remainder put away for future use.

Anguish swept over Ella as she tried to push back the resentment she felt toward her stepmother. *If Mama had been alive, we wouldn't be doing this.* Mattie, who was wise beyond her years, took Lura's hand, squeezed it, and smiled reassuringly back at Ella, sensing her thoughts. Ella suddenly realized her transgression and guiltily admonished herself for her grudge. I need to be strong too. Separation won't destroy our devotion to one another but will strengthen it. Ella smiled back and waved, holding Papa's hand on the platform as the wheels slowly began to pull the train car out of sight. It was then she heard a gasp from her father. As Ella looked up at his tearstained face, she found herself in the role of the encourager. "Oh, Papa, we'll be together again soon, you'll see. Don't cry. We'll find a way to bring them home!"

Later that afternoon
Little Rock, Arkansas

The carriage pulled up to a four-story brick building that looked immense to Mattie and Lura. Not understanding this to be their new living quarters, the girls remained seated, intimidated by its size, but admiring the framed arched porches and balconies that loomed large above them. The teacher struck her cane near Lura and motioned them both to follow her upstairs toward the front door.

Once inside, the matron of the dormitory greeted them with a warm smile as she sought to soothe any tension over their new surroundings.

"I'll see the girls to their room, Miss Malcom."

Simple signing such as eat, sleep, and get dressed began the girls' education at the school. As time progressed, Mattie and Lura quickly picked up sign language and made many new friends. But it was Mattie's precociousness that grabbed the attention of her teachers. To catch up on lost time for beginning her education so late, Mattie drove herself to extreme limits and soon surpassed those in her own class that had the advantage of starting their education at a younger age.

June 1898

Papa found a way to bring his girls home every summer. Over each successive season, both he and Ella gradually learned to sign to Mattie and Lura. This summer, Lura implored her papa's permission to stay home from the boarding school in the fall to help Mother Martha and Ella with the growing family. Reluctantly, he agreed. So it was Mattie alone, who made the train ride back to Little Rock that autumn.

Present day

"Grandma Libby, when was this picture taken?" asked Scarlett as she held the original picture of the sisters in her hand.

"Sweetheart, I'm not certain the year, but I know they're in their twenties because of the cameo pin on Mattie's blouse," she answered.

"Oh!" Scarlett cried. "I can see the pin clearly now."

"Dear, part of the cache in my collection is the book I mentioned earlier. The school wrote it in celebration of their first 125 years. Listen, while I read this early description: 'This institute is not an asylum, and weak-minded children cannot be received. It is not a poorhouse, and no one will be allowed to remain who has learned all it can teach. It is not a reform school. And should any prove incorrigibly vicious, after a trial, they will be discharged'" (History of Education Services, p. 30).

"There were two years in which monumental events happened in Mattie's experience at the school that propelled her life forward in ways she'd never imagined possible as a young girl. Here, take this book of history, Scarlett, and read for yourself what took place when Mattie went back to school in the fall of 1898," Grandma Libby said.

Scarlett sat in a cozy rocking chair inside her grandmother's office and turned to page eleven, chapter 6. "A great event happened on the campus of the Arkansas

School during this period. Dr. Alexander Graham Bell, the telephone inventor, and his deaf wife, Mabel, visited the school."

Scarlett couldn't help but imagine how Mattie must have felt when such a famous and important person came into her midst.

November 1898

"Supt. Yates, I'd like you to take me to the oral department so I may speak with some of your students. Then, I'd like to test the hearing of the group of pupils you've selected," Dr. Bell told him.

"By all means, this way, Dr. Bell," Mr. Yates said.

As Mattie assisted some of the younger students to be examined by the inventor, Mr. Yates said, "Mattie Henderson, here, is one of our brightest. She's excelled in all coursework during the short years she's been enrolled in this institution."

"I see. When Mrs. Yates and my wife return from their tour of this fine city, have Miss Henderson meet us in your office for some conversation," Dr. Bell said.

Later that evening

Dear, Papa,

I had the most gratifying experience today. Dr. Alexander G. Bell and his wife toured our school and tested a select group of students. Supt. Yates assigned me to help with some of our most recently enrolled while Dr. Bell administered tests. In midafternoon, I was summoned to the superintendent's office and introduced to Dr. Bell's lovely wife. We had a fascinating conversation in sign language. She asked me what goal I aspired to in life, and I said unequivocally: to teach the deaf. Dr. Bell explained Gallaudet College in Washington, DC, has a fine program to train teachers. He stated promising students from all over the country attend Gallaudet and receive the foremost training in deaf education.

Oh, Papa, is it too much to have such a grand hope? How could I go so far away from the family? It's one thing to be sixty miles from home, but our nation's capital must be over a thousand! I'm sure nothing will come of it, but I couldn't help being honored by his suggestion.

Your devoted daughter,
Mattie

Scarlett turned in the book to chapter 7 and read the title: "Disaster, September 30, 1899." *Here's what I wondered about earlier. And Mattie was right there!* she thought. "What was once the handsomest view in the state of Arkansas was a desolate scene of ruin when the sun rose yesterday morning. The fire which broke out at 2:00 a.m. at the Deaf-Mute Institute burned itself out by 5:00 a.m. after destroying everything in its reach." The Arkansas Gazette, October 1, 1899.

As she turned the page, Scarlett saw the picture of the Victorian girls' dormitory where Mattie lived, taken before the inferno. *Thank goodness she escaped in time,* Scarlett thought. She read how the only conveyance to reach the school from the firehouse was a hook and ladder wagon, whose passage was made more difficult when it plowed through mud and steep hills. Though no lives were lost the entire school grounds had been demolished.

Scarlett could only imagine.

September 30, 1899
1:45 a.m.

Mattie tossed and turned on her pillow as she dreamt the same recurring dream. It always started on a train with the blur of images outside a window going faster, faster, as the motion never stopped. She felt trapped in the runaway train and reached for the sliding door to run, tell the porter, when, opening her eyes she realized it was just a dream. Only this time, did she faintly remember Mama sitting beside her in the train car? *I need to get up and pour myself a glass of water. Perhaps read the next chapter in my Dickens novel,* she thought.

Mattie descended the stairs to the kitchen but paused on the landing to look out the window. *Is that fire I see coming from the main building across campus? Yes! I must wake everyone before it spreads this way!*

Six months later
One luminous evening

"Papa, the results of my entrance exams were scored, and I passed! I'll be able to attend Gallaudet in the fall of next year. Supt. Yates explained an anonymous donor provided the award all the way to my degree completion! Can you believe it?" Mattie signed to him.

"Yes, I can believe it, Mattie. I'm so proud of you. I only wish your mother was here to see this day." Papa signed back as he looked up into the night sky with its myriad of stars shining above.

He pulled out his pocket watch and noted the time, then signed, "Mattie, it's a quarter past nine, and look at the moon. It's smiling down on us. You know, sweetheart, even though you may be a thousand miles away, look up at the night sky and remember the same moon you see there, I'll see here at home. Let's agree, whenever possible, on a clear night; look to the moon at a quarter past nine, and we'll say a prayer for each other."

"Oh, Papa," signed Mattie, "what a perfect idea. It will help me to know we share that moment. But the Standard Railway Time means I'll be an hour ahead of you."

"I already thought of that," signed Papa. "When you look up at 9:15, I'll witness the moon at 8:15. And be assured, I'm saying a prayer for my girl."

Mattie reached her arms around her father and tightly hugged him. She never felt more loved.

Gallaudet College
April 2, 1906

My dearest family,

In one month, I'll be giving my valedictorian speech at the graduation ceremonies. It's difficult to believe that five years have passed, and I'll soon be teaching at my old school. I've already received a letter from the new superintendent, Mr. Washburn, to meet with the staff upon my return and share highlights of my college experience.

Now I've saved the best news for last! It's this: The guest of honor at our graduation is none other than the president himself. President Theodore Roosevelt will give an address on the same podium as I, can you believe it?

Please say an especial prayer that I have courage when I sign my speech before the president.

Papa, I'll be looking to the night sky on May 6th! I understand it will be a crescent moon.

All my love to each of you,
Mattie

Present day

"Grandma Libby, what's inside the little box with Mattie's file?" Scarlett asked.

"Well, let's take it out and see," her grandmother replied.

While Scarlett sat on the sofa, Grandma Libby went into another room and brought back a small box. She sat next to her granddaughter and read the gold print on its cover, "J. J. Livingston Jewelers, Conway, Arkansas. Open it, Scarlett, you might be surprised by what's inside."

Scarlett slowly opened the maroon case, and to her delight rested the most beautiful cameo she'd ever seen. "It's Mattie's, isn't it?" Scarlett said. "The one she's wearing in the picture."

"You're right," Grandma Libby replied. "Isn't the carving exquisite? With a beautiful girl sitting on a crescent moon to represent the pledge her father made to her."

"Oh, so this is the very one from her father?" Scarlett asked.

"Why yes, his graduation gift to her. That's how I knew when the picture was taken because she's wearing this cameo," Grandma Libby answered. "And someday I want you to have it, Scarlett, for showing such an interest in your ancestors."

"Grandma Libby! How can I ever thank you?" Scarlett said.

"You don't have to dear. Just pass down the story of how it came to you for future generations," Grandma Libby answered.

"Oh, I will grandma, but tell me, I'm curious, did Mattie truly teach at the deaf school in Little Rock?" asked Scarlett.

"Why yes, she did for many years. Until she met someone very special whom she married, but that's another story," Grandma Libby said.

******

Mattie Henderson was my great-great-aunt and the sister of my great-grandmother, Ella Henderson. Along with her younger sister, Lura, she attended the Arkansas Deaf-Mute Institute, now known as the Arkansas School for the Deaf. Her exemplary performance in school allowed her to attend Gallaudet College from 1901–06, and graduate as valedictorian of her class. After requesting documents from Gallaudet University Archives, I was sent her entrance exam papers, a printed copy of her speech, and a copy of the program listing President Theodore Roosevelt addressing the graduation class.

I couldn't have written this story without the material I received from the Arkansas School for the Deaf as well as archival records from Gallaudet University. Both sources served as inspiration and illumined to me events that took place in the life of this extraordinary woman—Daisy Margaret Henderson.

Bennett's Discovery

Present day

"GRANDMA LIBBY, WHERE did you get this rock?" Bennett asked as he cupped it carefully in his palm.

The fossil seemed sculpted out of an ordinary shell found along a seabed, but ancient all the same. Bennett traced its form with his finger in fascination.

"Why, Bennett, I unexpectedly came across the fossil in Grandpa's garden several years ago. One evening just as the sun was about to set, I decided to pick some spinach for a salad when I noticed it wedged between the rock wall and Grandpa's spinach greens. I couldn't believe how fortunate I was since years before as a college student, I'd searched countless times for a perfectly formed fossil, only to find fragments instead. I carried my perfect specimen inside, cleaned off the loose dirt, and tucked it away in a drawer for safekeeping."

Bennett turned it over in his hand then asked, "Do you know how old it is, Grandma Libby?"

"That I can't tell you," she answered, "but I found it odd that no ocean is close by, yet it speaks of a time when water once filled our property. Even fossils like this declare a story hidden away in the past. You know, Bennett, I like to think it was no accident I stumbled upon this relic. It serves as an emblem, my emblem. Just as fossils left in the ground are windows to open and reveal earth's story in history; in the same way, our ancestors leave traces of their lives behind for us to discover. And if there's one thing I love to do, it's to unravel stories of those who've gone before us."

Bennett looked out the window at the rock wall that divided the lawn and Grandpa's garden. Grandma Libby smiled as she knew what he was about to ask.

"Grandma, may I walk along the wall?"

"Yes, of course, but be careful not to disturb Grandpa's plants," she answered.

Tulips adorned one side of the earthy, stone barrier in reds and yellows dressing the background with color as Bennett made his way over the yard. Glancing toward the pond in the distance, he noticed Grandpa scatter feed for his prized hens. Their heads jerked up and down in a flurry of motion while they followed Grandpa's every step. Bennett reached the wall and balanced gingerly along its top, but realized he wasn't close enough to observe buried treasures he imagined beside it. He jumped down and dug his hands between the plants in hopes of finding a fossil as good as Grandma Libby's. After several minutes with nothing but jagged bits of rock and dirt for his efforts, he decided it was time to go inside and ask her what she meant about ancestors who left behind stories for us to unearth.

******

A window in time soon to be opened for Bennett to view.

11:00 a.m.
November 11, 1918
Front lines of France

All was suddenly quiet. No more shots, no more gas, nothing. It was over.

Corporal Hobson and his fellow doughboys poured into No Man's Land along with the enemy to celebrate. Shaking hands, slapping shoulders, cheering, and exchanging souvenirs were at once pandemonium. In an instant it all changed, and the corporal found himself before a man he could easily have fired upon the previous hour. Language was no barrier. As if brothers, they pulled out photographs, reached inside their pockets and exchanged tokens to lodge this moment as a lifetime memory. Corporal Wallace K. Hobson relinquished his favorite pipe he'd bought in England eight months before while his counterpart pressed something round into his right hand.

"Danke," said the German soldier with a broad smile.

"Thank you," Corporal Hobson said in return, and as quickly as they were together, just as quickly were they lost among the sea of soldiers that weaved through the crowd.

Later that evening, Corporal Hobson lay on his side when he felt an object hard inside his hip pocket and remembered the German soldier had given him something. In the melee, he'd forgotton about it until now when his body craved long, overdue sleep. He looked at the gift and realized he received the better end of the trade, only to marvel the man would part with such a keepsake. The passage of time would prove his conjecture correct, but he felt a deep obligation to protect the treasure now placed in his hands. It would be years before his mind forged an idea to return a favor with the same intent. Even so, circumstances and time work in tandem with life to architect the perfect moment for just as symbolic an exchange. And years later, long after Corporal Hobson was no longer soldiering, that ideal opportunity fell into his lap.

Present day

"Grandma Libby, how did you get so interested in history?" Bennett asked.

"I think it started when I was about your age, Bennett. My grandmother used to tell me stories her grandmother passed down to her. Over the years, I recorded and wrote down not only interviews with my grandparents but my great-grandparents, as well as aunts and uncles. Oh, Bennett, when I look back, I only wish…" her voice trailed off. He witnessed his grandmother lost in thought as she shook her head and stared off into space.

"What do you wish, Grandma Libby?" he asked.

"My dear, it took me years to hone my question techniques. Just think, when I was your age, and my great-grandmother was still alive, I could've asked her questions about her grandmother who was born in 1818! Now if that grandmother told my great-grandmother stories about her grandmother, she would've reached back to 1750!" she answered.

"But I thought you said you interviewed your great-grandmother?" he queried.

"Oh I did, Bennett, but I was young, and my questions back then were vague; not designed to whittle out nuggets of information to open a window into their world." She paused. "When you interview relatives about the past, try to pose questions that allows them to paint a picture in words." she said.

"How's that possible?" Bennett wanted to know.

"Let me see," Grandma Libby said, then continued, "After lots of trial and error conversing with ancestors, I changed my tactics to pose questions like this: Big Mom, open the door of your house on Magnolia Street, and tell me what you see; on the walls, in the bookshelf, or inside the medicine cabinet. You know Bennett, I can still picture Big Mom over a mound of bread dough. Her eyes closed, with memories about to pour out scenes in words as she pushed, then breathed her dough to perfection."

"Oh now," she patted Bennett's shoulder. "Talking about Big Mom's rolls makes me hungry. How 'bout I let a batch rise while I fix us some dinner?"

Bennett hugged her and ran out the door as Grandpa called him to help gather eggs from the hen house.

Later over their meal, Grandpa asked for a second helping of rolls when Grandma Libby said, "Bennett, hand us the pan from the stove will you, but be careful, it's still hot."

Grandpa leaned over toward Bennett, and in a loud whisper said, "Your Grandma Libby has a story for nearly everything in this house. Even the pan she cooked the rolls in; don't get her started about her Big Papa Hobson, who watched over German prisoners during World War II. Otherwise, we'll be here 'til midnight!" he teased.

"Oh, Curtis Walter, I've bored Bennett enough today. Now, why don't you two go outside while I clean up? Bennett can play in the tree house, and you can pick some beets for tomorrow's dinner," she said.

The tree house was Bennett's favorite place to be when he visited his grandparents. Grandpa positioned it between two large conifers to shade a balcony on one side and a windowed tower on the other. It was the perfect place to hide from an imagined enemy, listen to sounds of nature, or view constellations with his mounted telescope. From a perch, Bennett focused his eyeglass on a red-tailed hawk riding a wind current to the west. Behind him came the sound of digging. *It's the black knight!* he thought. *He must be trying to dig a tunnel to my hideout!* He refocused the eyeglass toward the noise. *No, it's only Grandpa hoeing weeds in the garden.*

"Bennett, I've put something in your mailbox with written instructions. I expect you to follow them," his Grandma Libby called from below.

"Sure," he answered while he pulled on the rope that drew the mailbox up into his fort. When he opened it, he noticed some folded brown, crumpled paper with burned edges, like a pirate's treasure map. It tickled him his grandmother made games out of the most ordinary things.

The message read: "Don't lose track of time and stay there too long, dear. You must to go to bed in an hour, but first you'll need to take a bath and put out clothes for church tomorrow. Your mother's singing a solo, and we should get there early. Love, Grandma. P. S. I've also enclosed a clue for your bedtime story."

Bennett turned the paper over to look for any hint that might jump out at him but saw nothing written. *How could I have missed it?* he wondered. Then he reached his hand back inside the mailbox and discovered a watch. Not a wristwatch, but an old, silver, pocketwatch without a chain. The dial was gold with large black digits, but the outer case was scratched from years of wear. Bennett situated it on the window ledge and went back to see if the hawk still circled the sky. He guessed Grandma Libby would explain how the watch was a clue for the story she'd tell; however now, he wanted to take advantage of any daylight left.

8:30 p.m.

"Grandma Libby, how was this a clue?" Bennett asked as he laid the old silver timepiece on a nightstand beside her.

"Well, dear, I'm sure you realize it helps us to stay on schedule in the present as well as plan for the future. When I wrote you needed to be inside within the hour, you had to be mindful of your time and rely on the watch to follow directions. Can you think of another reason a watch might be a clue?" she asked.

Bennett was silent a moment then spoke, "I think it's because you like to tell stories about the past. So tonight's story might be going back in time?"

"A good deduction," she said. "However, I'm not going to tell tonight's tale. I have a special treat for you. Many years ago, I recorded my Big Papa Hobson on tape. Then, after cassette tapes became outdated, I converted it to a disc to be used in more current devices. Tonight, I'm only going to play a portion of it for you. In the end, you might be surprised to learn why the watch became a clue. But first, let me give you a little background about my Big Pop."

Bennett's hair, still damp from his bath, lingered with the scent of mint shampoo. He laid down eager to hear what his grandma was about to tell him. On the edge of the bed, Grandma Libby adjusted knobs on an electronic device while a wallpapered scene in the background displayed patterns of a colonial-attired trio near a gazebo. She turned back to him and said, "Bennett, my Big Papa truly watched over German soldiers captured during World War II just as Grandpa mentioned at the dinner table. They were imprisoned at the Pine Bluff Arsenal in the 1940s. In a casual conversation with Big Mom one day she told me the pan she cooked her rolls in came from a German prisoner Big Papa had known. So the first time I used my tape player for an interview was the very day she suggested I try it out on Big Pop. It's much too long to play his entire story, and we've not much time before you go to bed, so I'll start it right after I asked him, 'Will you describe what you did at the prison camp?' Not only did he answer that question, but he revealed another surprise I never knew about him. It only took a little prodding to bring more of his stories to the surface. Are you ready?" she asked.

Bennett nodded yes and could see the mutual anticipation on his grandmother's face.

She turned on the recording and a deep voice began: "Libby, I worked on the day shift up at the arsenal. It wasn't hard work, but my chief duty was to keep an eye on prisoners in the canteen and mess hall. Sometimes in the spring and summer, I'd patrol those that worked in the fields as well."

Bennett could hear strikes on a windup clock in the background, and then Big Papa's voice continued.

"We were careful to follow the Geneva Convention, and the prisoners were paid in script when they worked in the fields or bakery."

"What's script, Big Papa?" Libby asked.

"The best way to explain it is, it's a substitute for legal tender. They'd use it in the canteens to buy cigarettes and such. 'Course we couldn't allow 'em to have real currency, or the ones who might attempt escape could've found their way to Mexico or beyond. That reminds me of the two Jerrys who did try to run for it, though." Big Papa said.

In the recording's background, Bennett heard water pouring from a faucet with the clamor of silverware sorted inside a kitchen drawer. He recognized the voice of a much younger Grandma Libby when she asked, "What do you mean by two the Jerrys who ran for it?"

"Why, I'd been over there in the first war, you see," Big Papa continued. "I refer to 'em as Jerrys because that's what we called 'em back then. Anyway, they had a search going on in all the surrounding counties for those two escapees. The local sheriff rode out with me down here in Cleveland County. He and I were the ones who found 'em over near Kingsland. They were scratched up from running and hiding in brush. One could speak English pretty well, and he was awfully worried what'd be done to 'em once we turned 'em over. We let 'em sweat a little bit, but 'course in the back of our minds we knew we'd honor regulations. 'Cause if they'd caught our boys in a similar circumstance, we'd hope they'd do the same."

A scratchy noise interrupted the interview. Bennett looked over at his grandma. She nodded and held her finger to her mouth to signal there was more.

"No, I well remember that captive who spoke English. He took my treatment of him as a kind gesture, I guess, 'cause on another occasion, he approached me holdin' a pan filled with rolls he'd made in the camp bakery. He wanted me to take 'em home, pan and all. Then I got to tellin' him about a German soldier I met years before. He seemed amused with my story of how we exchanged the first thing we pulled from our pockets. And that's when I got an idea.

You see, the day came when the war was over, and it was time to repatriate those prisoners back to Germany. On my last day at the camp, I helped process the return of confiscated possessions to 'em. When this soldier came forward, I took from my jacket, the pocket watch I'd been given years before and handed to him. At first, he refused my gift, but I said, 'No, it came from Germany. Now it should go back to Germany, and I want you to have it.'"

******

Quietly, Grandma Libby turned off the CD player, winked at Bennett and finished, "Now you know why the pocket watch was my clue."

She kissed him good-night, and whispered, "Sweet dreams."

Wallace K. Hobson, the author's grandfather, was drafted in WWI but didn't serve due to the war ending prior to basic training. He did, however, work at the Pine Bluff Arsenal during WWII in some capacity. The pan, used in the camp bakery, was given to Wallace by one of the German soldiers. The author still uses it today for baking Big Mom's homemade rolls.

Bibliography

Peter's Discovery:

1. Davidson, Chalmers. *Piedmont Partisan*. Davidson College (1951 edition), 23.
2. Davidson, Chalmers. *Piedmont Partisan*. Davidson College (1951 edition),184.

Wyatt's Discovery:

1. Colossians 2:12. *King James Version*.
2. Author unknown.
3. Deuteronomy 32:7. *King James Version*.

CPSIA information can be obtained at www.ICGtesting.com
Printed in the USA
LVOW10s0531300716

498224LV00006B/9/P

9 781681 643410